The One That Got Away

for Finn McClure

The One That Got Away

Zoë Wicomb

Five Leaves Publications
www.fiveleaves.co.uk

The One That Got Away
by Zoë Wicomb

Published in 2011
by Five Leaves Publications,
PO Box 8786, Nottingham NG1 9AW
www.fiveleaves.co.uk

First published in South Africa
by Umuzi, Roggebaai in 2008

Published in the United States by The New Press.
The story "Raising the Tone"
has been added to the original collection

ISBN: 978 1 907869 04 4

Five Leaves acknowledges
financial support from
Arts Council England

Five Leaves is represented to the trade
by Turnaround and distributed by Central Books.

This edition not for sale in
North America or South Africa.

Cover photograph of the Doulton Fountain in Glasgow
© Renee MacKenzie, www.reneemackenzie.com

Typeset and designed by Four Sheets Design and Print
Printed by Imprint Digital in Great Britain

Contents

Boy In A Jute-Sack Hood

Grant Fotheringay is at a loose end. These are his own
words. He has said them aloud, and now having struggled
with the new-fangled coffee machine, he paces the length
of the room that Stella — bless her bloody cotton socks —
called the lounge. He is alarmed: that is what *old* men do,
mutter to themselves. So there's nothing for it, such a
malarkey must be confronted head-on since the
unexamined life etcetera ... Defining his condition, raking
over his thoughts, over his own words, has become habit,
the old ballast that chains the dog etcetera ... There
seems to be no accounting for the words that slither into
the mind, and then he is duty-bound, owes it to himself —
because you are worth it, as the ads declare — to
investigate, which is to say poke, even if it is with a
retractable ruler, gingerly, at that writhing tangle of
decanted worms.

What then does it mean to be at a loose end? Grant
thinks images: a rope dangling from a mizzen sail; the
frayed edge of fabric, something rough like jute; the
forlornness of something or other; and he sighs
theatrically, at the unfinished that passes itself off as
freedom or enticement. He supposes, as he stands in front
of the window, waiting for the kettle to boil, that his arms
are dangling. Then, before him, like a vision, a child
charges across the lawn, purposefully, a zephyr whose
arms, swivelled in their sockets, stretch out behind him.
The child's cheeks are puffed out. He is running
backwards, but with the confidence of one who knows the
terrain, knows where he is going. Grant steps back from

the window. Weird: it would seem to be the image of the child, an after-image of streamers taut in the west wind, that has brought to mind, as it does for the time-traveller, the notion of a loose end.

Loose ends belong to another country, another time. And when the rest of South Africa bangs on about memory, he is reminded that there is another history, one that has no truck with memory. But being at a loose end and seeing the child charge across the rain-spangled lawn bring an irrepressible image of himself as child charging with a kite on Glasgow Green, a picture no doubt puffed up, he thinks, by kail-yard tales, or rather, his scorn for kail-yard. Grant winces at the thought of a yard, and the mean space of a Gorbals close. That surely accounted for his childhood asthma, that close of fag-ends, hawked-up phlegm, and the smell of neeps and sprouts cooked to death, that squeezed the air from your lungs and made you wheeze. Then he knew nothing of mangoes, avocado pears, could not have known of the Queen of Sheba leading her soft camels widdershins round the kirk-yaird a full two decades later. Instead, there was the Green — vast, bright, defiant under a pewter sky — for a boy with a kite that soared like an eagle. Lucy in the sky-y with di-iamonds. His blood-red kite, a diamond with a tail, thumbed its nose at the Presbyterian sky, taunted that grey lid until it lifted and light came crashing through the cloud. Before his very eyes the Green buckled into fells and highveld where lions roared and flashed their yellow eyes in the bracken.

It was from the grand old derelict fountain on the Green, its cracked, blunt-nosed sculptures, that his dreams were fed. There a child from the Gorbals could escape to far-off lands via the terracotta tableaux of the colonies. He did not mind the broken meths bottles, the smell of piss and vinegary pokes of chips as he wandered around the peoples of the colonies. Trailing his red kite, he became an explorer, a discoverer of things that no Glaswegian had dreamt of; he wandered through weird vegetation, slew the giants of Africa and sailed off to India. He favoured the bearded man in the South African tableau with a gun by his side, and at his feet a sweet, odd-looking girl who would speak in a lovely sing-song voice, quite unlike the slags who smoked and cursed in the close. But best of all was the ostrich with a long snake-neck and full, soft feathers like the girl's bosom, an image that guided his hand at night under the blanket and brought wet dreams of coupling with a continent. The worn school atlas that he claimed to have lost, and for which his teacher demanded three shillings, he kept under the mattress, safe from the younger children.

Yesterday afternoon, and only three months late, Grant sent off his manuscript, a monograph of one hundred and thirty thousand, two hundred and seventeen words, the fruit of four years' research and painful writing; although the pain after the first draft had abated. It is his first-born. It is not surprising then, he consoles himself, that he feels at a loose end, even if he had expected something else, something at least distantly related to pleasure or relief. For two of those years, more or less after Stella moved out (Jesus, what timing, what a bitch), he has lived the life of a recluse, other than the minimal conversation with colleagues and necessary interaction with students. Now he supposes he will have to think of a new project — but not yet. First there should be a loosening off, a settling of the mind so steeped in the late-nineteenth century. Should he take a deep breath and join a gym? No, he is neither ready for the sweat of the middle-aged, nor for the lycra-clad limbs of youth.

On the cream sofa, wide as a boat, the red silk cushions are lined up into stiff lozenges just touching at the corners to form a row of diamonds, which makes the blood rush to his face with rage. Why should he have to put up with this, twice a week, after Poppie has been? Why should he have to struggle with a maid who insists on having her own way, her own aesthetic? he supposes. He rearranges the cushions into careless piles, as if they had been tossed from afar; he hates the orderly line that stands on tip-toe to attention. The girl must imagine that he doesn't care, doesn't know that the untidy tumble of red is no accident, and all because he is a man, yes that's what it's about. As a progressive who has long since given up on manhood, he resents the stereotype, for what else could it be that blinds the girl — or woman, he should say — to the plumped up cushions that she finds each time so obviously, so artlessly, arranged into random heaps?

The rain comes and goes. Grant Fotheringay stretches out on the sofa, but no sooner does he settle down with the *Mail & Guardian*, than the child again crosses the lawn from right to left. This time over his thin T-shirt the child wears a folded jute sack, the type in which sugar is sold in bulk. With one corner tucked like a lining into the other and slipped over his head, the sack is a cape with a peaked hood, which keeps him dry. This time with arms stretched before him and puffed-out cheeks, he describes a wide arc across the lawn, his left wing dipping dangerously before landing. Then the child seems to rebuke himself, for suddenly he straightens, sober, pensive, as his cheeks deflate; he is too old for such nonsense. From his pocket he draws a rolled-up exercise book, saunters over to the large picture window, and with book in hand measures its length in wide strides, twice, back and forth, as if he cannot believe his own findings. He makes a note in his book, possibly of the number of strides. The rain stops once again.

Light bounces off the window, so that glancing into the room the child sees only dark shapes, only furniture, he thinks. He presses his nose against the pane, curious about the interior that he is sure will be wonderful. He has puzzled over the wonky wrought-iron table with a fully rusted top and the frayed stuff of the wicker chair on the stoep. He knows the man to be rich and grand. Why then does he keep such ramshackle, such shameful old things?

Can the child really not see Grant? He sees what he expects to see. For months now he has known the man to work all day in the study at the back of the house that looks out at the mountain. Sitting with his back to the window, the man would not have seen anyone running across the lawn, backwards, without bumping into anything, or anyone peering into the living-room window.

Is the child staring at him? Grant flushes, doesn't know whether to stir. This is the sort of thing that Stella would have taken care of. When the rain starts beating against the window, the face spreads across the pane; the sugar-sack hood frames black eyes around which he has cupped his hands the better to exclude the glare. Heavens above, what insolence, and Grant leaps to his feet and goes to the window where the child now stares in horror before putting his palms over his eyes with shame. Grant taps at the pane and with a wave beckons him in.

When Grant Fotheringay came from Glasgow in 1984, he knew nothing about the academic boycott of South African universities. Which does not mean that he knew nothing of the world. He knew lots of other things: about the Union, the Empire, the miners' strike, the Irish Troubles, Thatcherism in all its Tory viciousness, and, of course, the snootiness of England. As a research student he had been on an anti-apartheid march through the city, although he could not help feeling that the centre being cleared of traffic on a Saturday morning was an indulgence on the part of students. Had Grant known of the boycott, would he still have come? That he cannot answer: it is no longer possible to tell.

Professor Stevenson, his new boss in Cape Town, spoke of Grant's moral courage. The boycott, he agreed, was ill-considered; such isolation would simply make the establishment dig in their heels, and of course it was detrimental not only to the progressive academic community but also to the very black population it claimed to protect. Grant winced at the word 'black': was it okay to call people that? The march, that if the truth were told was an attempt to get close to a fiery redhead from Edinburgh whose name he has forgotten, may not

11

have brought the calculated outcome, but here in Cape Town, unexpectedly, it came in handy. (Now it seemed possible that the redhead was rather mild-mannered, but he couldn't be sure.) In Stevenson's retelling, the march was cast in the plural, and there seemed little point in being pedantic, in saying that there had been only the one, or that he had felt somewhat foolish chanting in the streets: Maggie, Maggie, Maggie; Out, Out, Out, or: Barclays Bank, Barclays Bank; Out, Out, Out — or some such awkward thing that made the Barclaycard in his wallet migrate and lodge itself in his heart like a thrombus. There had, of course, been no need to say that he had applied for three posts in Edinburgh and Glasgow, all without success.

And so, without premeditation, Grant found himself at Cape Town in the role of activist. You will have to make allowances for us here in the boondocks of Africa, old Stevenson said humbly. Your radical European tradition no longer comes naturally to us. It's all uphill here, a struggle to hit the correct note of dissidence, he wheezed. Grant felt the gravity of the situation, the new responsibility, but there was, thank God, none of the unease of the Glasgow march where the redhead had thrust a Free Nelson Mandela placard with a photograph of a burly young boxer into his hands. Here in the brightness of the Cape sun or the cool shade of suburban gardens, the lines were clearly drawn. How could he be anything but heir to a liberalism that in the blinding southern light bled so wantonly into radicalism?

Before long, and by way of finding favour with younger firebrand colleagues who were known to have *toyi-toyied* through the coloured suburbs, the story gathered ambiguous mention of the ANC. He did not elaborate, but others assumed that the breaking of the boycott had somehow been sanctioned, that in the cloak-and-dagger climate of secrecy it would not do to ask questions. Wally Serote, what a speaker, what heroic figures those guys cut on the balcony of Glasgow's City Chambers! That was what he actually said, and Grant was surprised to find that such innocent mention of exiled revolutionaries brought awed respect. Again, it was the woman who had taken him along to some or other event where senior members of the banned organisation addressed the Scottish anti-apartheid movement. They spoke of Outspan oranges and economic boycott, but he does not remember any mention of academia, or perhaps Grant had slipped into daydreaming or had actually nodded off. He recalled staying up until the early hours with the redhead, all to no avail. He does not think he saw her again.

How much nicer it was anyway to find himself thawing in Cape hospitality, finding his political feet without the dubious guidance of sex. As he later said to Stella, it was his very own northern heart that he found in Cape Town, a healthy heart that turned out to be hungry for political challenge. Pah, so much for Stella's commitment. Where was she now that Rome was burning, or at least still smouldering? Well, in Edinburgh, of all places, which in some ways conveniently confirmed for him the permanence of his stay in the South. And was he not also entitled? Did he not in his own humble way, as did all the activists on the Jameson steps, contribute to the birth of the new South Africa?

The boy seems not to understand the man's gesture. He runs his hands over his eyes and over the tight fleece of hair under the sack, and disappears. Grant finds him squatting on his haunches on the back stoep, writing in a grubby notebook. He turns out to be older than Grant thought, eleven or twelve, although one can never tell with these people. He does not look up as the man towers over him, but there is nothing craven about the set of the thin shoulders, it is not even an act of bravado; the child is simply absorbed.

What are you doing? Grant asks.

Writing, he says. I'm writing down the names of bushes

13

and things in the garden, and then when I go home I'll see if I got them spelt right.

I could check them for you ... Grant is after all at a loose end, but no, the boy would like to do it himself, in his new dictionary. That is what he had wanted for Christmas and so this year Father Christmas managed to get to Grassy Park for a change. Then he smiles, I don't believe in Father Christmas; it was my dad. I don't believe in God either, but you're not allowed to say so.

His dad is George, the gardener who asked at the beginning of the year if the child could come along during the school holidays — he was a good boy, he would not be a nuisance — with the usual slyness of these people, for there was the child standing stiffly beside the father who no doubt thought that Grant could not refuse in his presence. Couldn't be left alone at home, George mumbled, although Grant seemed to remember that there were a number of children. But it would not do to ask. Better to just say yes rather than unleash a long, convoluted story that would not add up, that would have to be taken with a pinch of salt. Anyway, what did he care, with that bitch gone it hardly mattered as long as the child kept out of his way. And now, many months later, it turns out that the boy still comes on Saturdays although Grant has never seen him before.

So what's your name? he asks.

Samuel. And yours? the child asks without looking up from his writing.

Grant starts. Dr Fotheringay, he stammers, but the child says that he knows, that he also knows him not to be a real doctor, so what is his real name?

He repeats after Grant. Grant's a nice name, he says, solemnly intoning: Grant-us-thy-peace, and then as he returns to his writing, Dr Fotheringay has the distinct feeling of being dismissed.

Righty-ho then, he says, and wonders where on earth he had picked up that expression. Righty-ho? He is sure that he knows no one who says righty-ho.

When Grant returns to the back stoep an hour later the child has finished his writing. Still hooded in the jute sack, he is reading the editorial of an old *Mail & Guardian* salvaged from the pile at the back door.

Let's go inside, Grant says, no need to wait until you get home. You can use my dictionary to check your work.

Samuel folds up his sack neatly and carries it under his arm. In the study he lets out a wolf whistle at all the books. He goes along the shelf and ghost-runs his index finger down the spines, not touching; he reads aloud the titles, hesitating before unfamiliar words that he mouths silently before saying out loud. These he writes down in his exercise book; he will check the meanings later in the dictionary. Grant goes to the kitchen to prepare food, salad and left-over chicken. It would be a nice change to have lunch with someone, even with a strange boy. He nips into Stella's herb garden, now overgrown — he must have a word with George — where he finds some straggly chives for the salad.

Lunch, he calls to Samuel, let's have something to eat. He has set a festive table in the kitchen with woven mats and matching napkins, but Samuel says wait, he'll get something from the garden, and returns with a posy of fennel heads, rosemary and marguerite that he stuffs into a glass of water.

Daisy is my favourite, he says, I like the Namaqua daisy, the one that comes out in September. What's your favourite? he asks. Grant has none. He is unnerved by the boy who has made himself so curiously at home. How has he managed to make Grant uneasy in his own house? Thus the man boasts like a child: I'm not interested in the garden, just as long as it looks neat. I spend all my time in the study, reading and writing books. Samuel nods his approval. That's good, he says. When the boy finishes he places his cutlery neatly together and fidgets; he is anxious to get to the study. Grant asks if he doesn't like chicken. He should have said, then he could have had some ham instead. But Samuel says no, he has had plenty to eat; he left some chicken on his plate for courtesy's sake. It takes Grant a while to work this out from the boy's strong Cape Flats accent.

And so it comes about that Samuel spends Saturdays in the house. No longer is there the childish rushing about across the lawn or playing at being an aeroplane. He would knock on the front door and go straight to the study where Grant has moved a small table from a guest room for him. The boy is quiet as a mouse, reading and writing, and Grant, who has never tolerated anyone in his study, is surprised to find himself working perfectly well at his own desk. Over a protracted lunch Samuel quizzes his host on a range of topics, and Grant has to mind his Ps and Qs since the boy will often stop to take notes, and there is nothing worse than seeing your thoughtless or show-off comments fixed in writing. The boy promises to teach Grant his system of shorthand. He no longer leaves any food for courtesy's sake.

Once, after lunch, Grant asks if he would like to wash the dishes. Samuel furrows his brow theatrically. Would that not be inappropriate? he asks, clearly pleased with his use of the word, and Grant thinks it best to say yes, that perhaps it would. He says that if Dr Fother wants him to do some work Doctor must say so, but he would rather do jobs like taking the books from the shelves and dusting them. Grant says no, that he doesn't want him to do work of any kind, that's what Poppie is there for. He also doesn't like being called Doctor Fother, but can't find the words to say so.

Inappropriate. That was what his new friend, Jenny, said on the phone that morning. Saturdays at home had become sacrosanct; he would not go out for lunch with her party of friends, so that Jenny asked if Samuel's visits were not inappropriate. Inappropriate, he shouted, what a ludicrous thing to say. What's inappropriate about having lunch with a kid, and who cares about propriety anyway? Jenny said that some people did, and that he ought to be careful. He said he hoped that she was not

16

one of those people, that she had interrupted an interesting discussion on justice, and that he would like to be excused.

It is on a cold wet afternoon when they are in the kitchen for a coffee break, that there is a knock on the bolted lower door. Samuel had managed to get the cappuccino machine working, and Grant has put out slices of granadilla cake from the farm stall. It is George, leaning in over the latched lower door. He wonders if the Doctor shouldn't think again about where the new peach trees should go; he has an idea that they'd be better off along the southern fence. The Doctor must come and have a look. There'll be no problem shifting the rose bushes; they won't mind; they'll do fine on the other side by the jacaranda tree.

Righty-ho, Grant says. Could George wait just there while he fetches a rain jacket; he won't be long. George rests his forearms on the lower door. He must be taking in the sumptuous table, the tantalising smell of coffee, the posy of pale-blue plumbago, rosemary, and dark-eyed daisy, and the back of the boy whose eyes are fixed on the milky foam frothing above the rim of the coffee cup. How much more foam could the cup hold above its rim before it collapses down the sides? Samuel wonders, as he hears his father's breathing, hears the crunch of footsteps as his father turns away from the door to pace the back stoep until Grant arrives, zipping up his jacket. The rain pounds loudly on the roof.

The following Saturday Grant finds himself waiting, unable to concentrate on his new project on literature and ethics. Samuel has not turned up. Should he ask George where the boy is? From the window where he nurses an unusual lunchtime glass of wine, he keeps track for a while of George, a flash of blue overalls weaving in and out of the foliage, or hidden by shrubs, then appearing again to fuss over the peach saplings. Strange, how the man holds his head at an angle, just as the boy does. He would not be surprised if George were to whip out of his pocket a folded exercise book in which to make notes.

Grant pours the wine down the sink. He is, he supposes, at a loose end, in spite of the new direction his research is taking, and this time having a contract with an English university press. It is not until the following week when Samuel again does not turn up, that he decides to ask George. He has bought the boy's favourite caramel cake from the farm stall, and has himself collected and arranged daisies in a new crystal vase. Grant saunters to the far end of the garden where George, bending over a wheelbarrow, is preparing a mulch; he will speak to him about the peach trees.

They're doing well, George says. There should be a small crop of fruit next year.

Where's Samuel? Grant asks abruptly. George says that he's a funny boy, just gets an idea in his head and then he's hundred per cent behind it. Now it's *mos* the mountain. Last week Samuel announced that he and his friends would climb the mountain on Saturdays, just like that, out of the blue. George has not seen these friends before, and Doctor must now understand that they don't look like very respectable boys, but that Samuel is a headstrong somebody. From the library he got a huge pile of books on the mountain, just so high, and George holds his hand up at chest level. His mother's very very worried about him.

At four o'clock, as George struggles out of his overalls on the back stoep, Grant hands him a Woolworths bag to give to the boy but George, having peered into the bag, hands it back. He says thank you but it's okay, Samuel already got a thesaurus. Father Christmas brought it. Then he picks up the jute sack folded on the chair and says he will take that, that with all this unseasonable rain, the sugar sack will come in handy.

18

Disgrace

So Grace, what's your secret? asks Fiona, leaning against the doorframe.

Grace stares at her blankly; she had not been listening, had instead heard the echo of Tracy-Anne's week-old words over and over in her head — and now what's this nonsense about secrets. Where must she get time for such girls' talk? This woman doesn't stop, all kinds of strange talk, funny ways, and nosey too — heavens, there's no beating her for nosiness.

But I don't have secrets any more; I leave that kind of thing for the young people. They must sigh about love and cram their hearts with silliness that can't be said to other people. Me, I can say just anything at all — South Africa is *mos* now a free country.

No, Fiona says, the secret of looking so young and slim. Look at your fabulous skin, your figure, and your amazing energy; I mean, how do you manage at your age to rush about like this cleaning houses and ironing and things, and still look so wonderful.

She watches as Grace's head starts shaking, like the arm of a faulty clock, back and forth, cranking itself up to strike the hour.

Grace knows it's flattery, knows that she is past looking anything at all, although, even if she must now say so herself, she has always looked young for her age. Which is just as well. Young for seventy-four, to be precise, no one would guess, and she certainly is never going to let on, because why, that would just be the end of her job. But let there be no mistake: she's no fool to flattery.

No, you must just keep busy, that's what I say, that's what keeps you young.

But the woman doesn't give up; she stands in the door with a bowl of muesli, standing up, for heaven's sakes like a donkey, which can only give you indigestion, and chewing slowly, reluctantly, while she looks at her with a wry little smile, as if she can see right into Grace's head. The woman is still in her nightdress, low-cut, so that she has wrapped around her neck a scarf, which Grace must say is the most beautiful thing she has ever seen. Silk, she supposes, and in shimmering blues and greens that flow into each other, exactly the colour of the sea on Boxing Day, although she no longer gets to the sea. Even that Boxing Day trip has become too much like hard work. So Grace, you're not telling then? the woman persists. Grace has no idea what the secret could possibly be. This must be what the children call small talk, the white woman's idea of being friendly; she'll have to get this person off her back. Then lured, after all, into girls' talk by the prospect of taking a break from ironing, Grace straightens her back. Her head starts shaking again as she pecks about for words.

Okay, she says, the secret, come I'll tell you, she says, playing for time, the secret to good skin and hair is — and here she pauses — is plain cold water. Listen, once you get that water in the kettle and you heat it up, then all the goodness flies out. Water must be used just as it comes out of the tap, like sea water, you know. Yes, cold, and then on top of everything it saves you first lighting a stove and so on. It's that shock in winter when you splash your body with cold water, that's what does the trick. And in summer it's nice and fresh, you know, to shower with cold water and fix the skin. Me and my older daughter, Tracy-Ann, we shower the water over each other, and Miss must see, you should see how nice her skin also looks.

Grace's head stops shaking. Her story has the advantage of being the truth, but who would have thought that her cold-water wash, the thing of necessity, could pass for a cosmetic secret? She had figured it out for herself: cold water tightens the skin, and what's good for the skin must be good for the hair. Sometimes whilst cooking, with the bottle of fish oil within reach, she would *sommer* rub a bit of oil into her hands and face to relieve the tightness. But she says nothing of the cooking oil.

Ah, so that's it, says Fiona. I'll try that, the cold-water miracle.

As if the woman would. As if she, Grace, would fall for that fake talk. She can tell from those sweet-smelling bottles and silver jars that these fancy women are addicted to their expensive potions, their *toorgoed*, which like any *toorgoed* must be paid for, and still it doesn't work. Still they scour the shiny picture books for more beauty tips. So why, she wonders, did the woman ask? And why did she give in to the woman's nosiness and speak about such foolish things? It's like being unfaithful to her own name, making herself ungracious, when Grace is a name from no less than the holy book itself. Now she must just keep her mouth shut and say nothing of the fish oil or of never leaving the house without a hat. She takes up the Hoover and purses her lips.

Do you have a long way to go for water? Fiona shouts above the noise of the Hoover.

Oh no, we do have taps in Manenberg. What does the woman take her for?

I'd like to visit a coloured township. I could perhaps come and see you at home some time, Grace? For tea? she adds, as if that would make it better. Grace doesn't know what to say. She knows that now her silence is ungracious, but what can she do? Imagine, inviting yourself to tea. No, such a palaver would wear her out, and already she feels a wave of weariness lapping at her feet. What a business that would be on her day off, and with her china set all chipped now, no longer at its best. That woman will just have to do without, and she, Grace will hope for the best, hope that it's idle talk.

21

Grace thinks of Fiona as *that* woman. She is from overseas where they have funny ways, like using first names when they don't even know a person, although of course in Grace's case she is only the char and so that *is* her name, which is a pity, for with such a holy name it would be lovely to add a decent title: Miss Grace. As a young girl she used to mouth to herself in the cracked mirror, Miss Grace, and toss her hair, and her mother said, airs and graces, just see it doesn't all end in disgrace. Imagine, wanting to be called by your first name. Fiona, the woman said the first time, holding out her hand. No, I don't want to be called Miss McAllister; it takes too long anyway. And this time, the second time of visiting here by Miss Haskins, she even tried to kiss Grace, that puff-puff kind of kissing that the white people do. *Aitsa*, Grace had to be quick on her feet there.

My word, she told Tracy-Anne, I almost fell over with skipping sideways.The woman is too forward, and this nonsense of calling her by her name, she can forget it. Not that Fiona isn't a very pretty Christian name, and a pretty woman she is too, with real red hair that in the sunlight looks just like the Clairol girl's. Although she goes quite ugly with anger when Grace says, You English people from overseas ... I'm Scottish, Miss McAllister snarls, actually baring her teeth. Now what kind of putting on is that, she said to Tracy-Anne, when everybody knows it's the same place, same people. But Tracy-Anne said she should be careful, and *maar* play along, there'll be some reason or other for the woman's putting on, and then of course the girl saw her chance and said, Actually mummy must be careful; mummy doesn't know everything even if you think you do.

Always finds an opportunity to get at her, a real *geitjie* that older girl-child of hers is. And don't think she hasn't noted the disrespect, the 'you' and 'yours', slipping in. Ungrateful, that's what children are. You bring forth in sorrow and now years later you're still slaving away, and why? Because Tracy-Anne has her hands full with a no-good man, while she, Grace, has her hands full with the grandchildren. Children must *mos* look after their parents; Grace took care of her own mother, herself a *geitjie* at the best of times, until the day she died in her very own arms, but not Tracy-Anne, oh no, she has not a cent left over to pass Grace's way. Besides, she, Grace, wants nothing to do with that *dagga-roker* of a layabout husband. And as for her late-lamb, her Jane, how right she had been in sparing her the burden of a fancy double-barrelled name, for what good can come of it all now that the child, having got herself all the way to university, has settled for an unsuitable chap, an artist or something with no income, but intent on wasting what little he has on an expensive trip overseas. No, she can see it clearly: her tired old body in the wrap-around apron being carried out on a stretcher, the yellow duster dangling like a flag from her rigor-mortised hand, straight from Miss Haskins's house to her grave.

And so she didn't tell Tracy-Anne how last time the woman just disappeared back to England, straight from the Eastern Cape where she was visiting, didn't bother to come back to the house even though Miss Haskins was expecting her, and that poor soul — a kinder or more decent employer could not to be found in the whole Cape Peninsula — was bitterly disappointed. Yes, she left without saying goodbye, and what's more, without as much as a tip for Grace, when the blinking English pound is worth so many rands. It's of course not the money, it's the thought that counts, being appreciated and so on, but try saying that to Tracy-Anne and you'll just get an earful of something outlandish.

It was when the Scottish winter seemed to go on forever that a letter from her old school friend Shirley Haskins arrived. They had lost touch in the eighties when Fiona would not have considered visiting South Africa with its evil regime. Besides, it was such a hectic time under

23

Thatcher's misrule, the years of marches and demonstrations: trips down to Greenham Common, camping at Faslane, the miners' strike, and of course Fiona's most committed project, the anti-apartheid movement. Now, here she is in Cape Town on a second visit in Shirley's beautiful house, packed with what's called transitional art from the townships. Shirley is one of those clever people who, with no more than a glance, can tell whether a work is any good, and then she knows just how to display it. With the muesli bowl still in her hand, Fiona wanders around the room admiring the wood carvings and the artefacts made of telephone wire.

Grace looks up briefly, sympathetically; she cannot believe how easily these people from overseas are taken in. Just a load of old rubbish made by the layabouts and *dagga-rokers*, she says helpfully; they're nothing but *skelms* setting out to rob innocent people, especially the ones from overseas who've got now a lo-ot of money. Now, she could direct Miss McAllister to a chap who really is good with his hands, who makes toys and stuff with wire and old bits of tin that look exactly like the real things.

Shirley got in touch with her after the publication of Fiona's first book of poetry. I had no idea, Shirley said, that you were going to write, and Fiona said no, nor did she. It just so happened with the world settling down and with more time on her hands that she could be still, could think, and hey presto, it came out as poetry. Shirley said Fiona should come over; she could imagine no one appreciating the South African landscape more, and with Fiona's understanding of the country's history, its politics and economics, she surely could mine some poetry out of such splendid material.

Fiona said no, it would be presumptuous, she wouldn't dream of writing about a place she doesn't know intimately, hasn't lived in, but she would all the same like to see the Cape and travel through the Karoo with Shirley, with whom it was clear she had as much as ever in common. Perhaps now under a new dispensation,

South Africa was the place to be. Fiona had for some years felt something lacking. Having moved in 1990 from 'genteel' Edinburgh to 'gritty' Glasgow — she would wiggle in the air two raised forefingers of disavowal — in pursuit, she supposed, of that intangible thing, the West End for a while kept her diverted. From her living room window where she sat struggling with words, with the meaning of life, and the terrible responsibility for the planet's demise, the Botanic Gardens beckoned. And it was there in the Kibble Palace that she became acquainted with the flora of the Cape and sat in the tropical heat where the plop-plop of condensation did the trick and brought the refractory words stumbling head over heels onto her notebook. So surprising, they could have been in a foreign language, a parcel of words that arrived from abroad in the post. She tried not to think of the old regime, of the letter bombs and pretty parcels with explosives hidden in the centre. Then Shirley's letter arrived, just as she felt that the monocultural West End with its glass-and-stainless-steel coffee houses and gourmet food shops would no longer do, was indeed anything but 'gritty'.

Somewhere she had also kept a postcard from Grant Fotheringay, a politically naive young man she once fancied against her better judgment. That was way back in her Edinburgh days, but she had given up on him, had to admit to herself that the man had ice in his veins and cared nothing for her, and so years later she was surprised by the postcard. The message said that he was lecturing in Cape Town, and that that day he voted for the first time, along with the oppressed people of South Africa.

Fiona had kept the card purely for the picture, captioned at the back as 'Wall decoration — The Three Hunters — traditional skills incorporating contemporary ideas'. She found it without difficulty, and examined again the photograph of a traditional Venda house with thatched roof, painted white and ochre in decorative scallops.Three identical clay figures dangled long, parallel legs over the wall of the homestead. Their torsos were foreshortened, as if below, immediately behind the wall, there was a hidden bench on which the male figures were actually seated, with thighs raised, and knees resting on the wall over which their legs dangled. Each wore a hat and held in his hands something (the clay moulding was rough), a fan-tailed bird perhaps, that reached up to the shoulder. To their left, on the same wall, was a bas relief of a gun pointing at a wiggly blue-and-white spotted snake. Traditional skills! Fiona laughed out loud. She imagined revolutionaries fobbing off the neighbouring white farmers with a story of hunters, the stiff formality of the shortened figures passing off as folk-naive style. She knew that Grant too would have seen the hunters' bearing as military, an illegal depiction of armed resistance, the catch ambiguously batoned against each left shoulder like a gun, standing in for a gun, and the actual gun on the wall, innocent and *faux-naïf*. How the people must have split their sides at the slapstick of stern soldiers with their hidden bottoms, a code that the boers had failed to crack. Fiona would like to find that village in Venda, see if the tableau is still there, now surely a monument to freedom. She would also not mind seeing the Fotheringay man again.

Grant Fotheringay, in spite of having shed the awkwardness of his youth, or perhaps because of it, was a disappointment. He had put on weight; he wore a belt, as if the trousers that cut somewhat into his stomach were in danger of slipping down. He remembered sending the postcard on the very day of the elections, but no, he had not thought the image in anyway subversive, so that Fiona was embarrassed about her interpretation: zealous and gushing, he no doubt thought, and he was, after all, the expert in reading.

Grant had kindly arranged a party at a restaurant, a stiff affair of academics who reminded her of nothing less than the clipped white world of middle England. It would seem, she said, that the Scots necessarily lose their way in the old colonies; but no one knew what she meant. Grant explained that whereas people were plain poets in the rest of the world, in Scotland they were Scottish poets. Thus he and she skirmished, faltering like foreigners at a ceilidh, and the guests, puzzled, broke off into whispered conversations. It was then, Grant told her about Pringle, the father of South African poetry, a Scot she had never heard of. It was, Fiona knew, Grant's way of skirting the subject of her own poetry, but she appreciated the lecture all the same. She would do some research on Pringle, who, it seemed to her, was unusual in that he found rather than lost his way in the colony. That may well explain, Grant said wryly, why he returned to England rather than to Scotland. Puzzled by his bitterness and in particular his irrational hatred of Glasgow, Fiona resolved not to see him again.

When Shirley returned to Cape Town after their amazing trip to the Karoo, Fiona stayed behind in Prince Albert. She would go on to the Eastern Cape to explore Pringle country. Literary tourism was, of course, naff; nevertheless, feeling drawn to the man who founded the spirit of freedom in the colony, she wanted to get to know the old district of Albany. Shirley was disappointed. She had planned a number of jaunts in Cape Town, and there was still so much to show.

Fiona promised to spend the last two days back in the city but, as it turned out, she was held up in Grahamstown and drove straight to the airport where she barely caught her plane. I'll be back next year, she consoled Shirley on the telephone.

But Shirley was not to be consoled. How is one to bear it, she dolefully asked Grace, when you finally find a soulmate, and then next thing — she threw her hands up in despair — she's gone? She tapped out on the fingers of her left hand: there's still the wine route, I had planned, then a picnic at Silvermine, and of course swimming with

27

the penguins at Boulders. Had Grace ever done that? Grace felt for her, so she didn't say about the police on that Boxing Day, oh years ago when Ed was still alive, beating them off the beach with wooden batons. How were they to have known that the beach had in the meantime been declared white? As for penguins, she didn't think there were any; they must have come for the white people who were so pleased to swim with them. Oh I used to swim like a fish in my time, Grace boasted instead. We always used to go to the beach on Boxing Day, but nowadays it's more trouble than it's worth packing your things and risking your lives on that blarry train full of *skollies*, and when you get there the *dagga-roker* spoils everything, and Tracy-Anne gets upset, and the children scream, and then all hell breaks loose. Oh, Miss Haskins *mos* know how they torment her.

But now Miss McAllister is back, on her second visit. There is talk of her buying a house in Cape Town, and she just hopes that the woman does not let Miss Haskins down again. Grace for one is not going to allow her to come to tea in Manenberg. Miss Haskins had clearly been pressed into asking. Grace can tell from the roundabout, half-hearted way Miss Haskins said that the woman wants to see how other people live, but Miss Haskins knows that that would be too much of a palaver for her, although it is not a good idea to say how tired she is; she must be careful not to give away her age. No, she just had to be straight: Miss Haskins must please explain that there is nothing so special to see, that tea tastes no different in Manenberg — the water is from the same reservoir.

It is the English woman's last day and what a to-do. Miss Haskins is behaving like a teenager, mooning about with moist eyes. Nobody knows Miss Haskins better than Grace does, and she can see that this overseas person has brought big trouble, cause if ever she'd seen anyone in love then it's now her missus. In this new South Africa people get up to all kinds of things, even the coloured girls in the township are at it, falling in love with other girls, and although Grace knows it to be disgusting she can't help feeling that she'd rather Tracy-Anne's *dagga-roker* were replaced by a girl. She wonders if the woman knows the trouble she is causing, what with her puff-puff kissing and leading innocent people up the garden path.

Grace remembers to ask if Miss McAllister wants any ironing done; one thing about her now is that she doesn't hold any grudges, as a professional one doesn't let your personal opinions get in the way.

No thanks, the woman says, but Grace persists.

It's not nice to pack crumpled things, she advises. You never know when you'll have an accident: your bag flies open and then every busybody in the world gets a good look at your things. And unironed things may declare themselves clean on a washing line, but in a suitcase, no there they always look like dirty washing.

Och no, the woman says, I'll do the ironing myself, when I get home. Things will only get creased. Then she hums and hahs, she could do it now, but no she'd rather do a final turn in Long Street before meeting Shirley for their farewell drink, and she shoves her clothes into the bag.

Grace knows exactly what that's all about. Meanness — the woman doesn't want Grace to do the ironing so she needn't leave a tip. And with all those rich English pounds too, it's unbelievable, no wonder she calls herself Scottish. Grace, who will be gone by the time she comes back for her bag, holds out her hand stiffly as the woman approaches; she is certainly not going to be kissed goodbye.

Grace does not mean to look in the woman's suitcase. She takes to the room an ironed shirt that must have got mixed up with Miss Haskins's laundry, and that is the very moment when she feels faint. It's not the first time. Probably the heat and the fact that she hasn't slept at all well last night. Since the bed will in any case have to be stripped, she sits down, puts her head on the embroidered pillowcase and shuts her eyes. For a moment the room seems to swirl around her, so that she holds onto the edge of the open suitcase to steady herself. Her fingers catch on a pile of pink jersey — lovely stuff, soft as a baby — which in turn yanks to the surface the swirling blues and greens of a scrap of silk. Then the world grows miraculously still. As if mesmerised, she tugs at the fabric, watches it snake through the tangle of garments as she lifts it out of the bag. Grace rises, holds the scarf in both hands, runs it through her fingers, and in the glorious silence hears the swish of silk, the rush of water, of the tide foaming over shiny wet boulders. Her fingers work deftly; they fold the fabric into a small square and slip it into her pocket.

Grace leaves without finishing the ironing.

She is still awake at midnight, amazed by the woman who has taken a silk scarf that does not belong to her, and wonders what to do. She rolls away from the child who shares the bed, and slides out to grope in the dark for the thing she has taken, the exquisite thing she has taken for herself. Not stolen. She is not a thief; she has never in her life stolen anything. She should take it back. But to whom? She could throw it away, into the fire, drown it, but with the McAllister woman now gone, what would be the point?

Grace wraps the scarf around her neck. She would like to see herself in the mirror. It is hers; she is entitled to it; did she not hand-wash the woman's silk shirts, change her bed, polish her floor? It is hers until the woman phones to let Miss Haskins know, and then Miss Haskins will be furious, will say that it's a mystery, a mistake, that her Grace would never do such a thing. Or, as she looks Grace in the eye, she will see the years stamped on her face and say enough is enough, that Grace-the-thief is too old, that she should go — go and put her feet up. It is when the other child, asleep on the floor, coughs and grunts, that Grace starts. Shame rises hot like hives in her neck so that she whips the scarf off. Of course, she must take it back and confess her sin.

Grace arrives at work to find Miss Haskins in a rush. She is on her way out, has no time to talk, waves impatiently at Grace.

Later, it will have to wait, she says, and flying across the hallway points to an envelope on the table. For you, from Fiona.

Grace feels the great weight of her years. She throws the scarf onto the table and sits down to examine the letter. Her hands shake as she draws a crisp one-hundred-rand note from the envelope marked with her name, marked 'Miss Grace' in bold black capitals — Miss McAllister's wee mockery of the way things are done here. Grace feels her head shaking, back and forth, feels the shame rising from her scalp as if each hair is being uprooted, one by one, leaving her bald as a baby. It is, dear God, just as her mother said: from airs and graces comes disgrace.

The One That Got Away

Drew has kept mum. Not a word, he had promised himself, would he breathe to anyone, not even to his clever Janie, because cleverness does not always come in handy with such projects. Janie is a no-nonsense person, not given to flights of fancy, and that, he knows, is why he has fallen for her. But he will not risk a discussion; there is the danger of her thinking the work childish and, although he doesn't have a clear idea of what this project is all about, he does know that secrecy is crucial to guarding plans that are still in their infancy, to thinking things through.

Drew admits to a boyish sense of adventure that takes him back to the drowsy afternoons at high school where Mr Wilton the history teacher settled in his chair with legs wide apart to read aloud from the textbook. Then the boy drummed his heels on the floor to quell the need to escape, had to imagine a pair of strong hands pinning down his shoulders, for the voice of the man ventriloquising Fowler & Smit brought an irrepressible urge to run. His pulse quickened at the thought of running, breathless, without stopping, to the rim of the disk that was the real world where, looking down, newness would lie sprawling before him in another disk, spinning like a polished coin around the sun. Had he been an athlete he would have leapt and landed in that alien landscape: mountain ranges with high snow-capped peaks, trees burning in autumnal colours that he had seen only in pictures, colours so distant and so subtle that they had never been named. He would have been the one that got away. And all the time old Wilton was reading aloud in a dominee's voice the sentences that had to be memorised for the examination, and that the class had to underline in their Fowler & Smit, now reduced to roughly half the history. Stick to the facts, and underline neatly, with a ruler and in pencil, Wilton said, as a mark of respect for the book, since pencil being erasable, did not deface. All marks made in a book in ink was vandalism.

Drew used five colours of ballpoint pen and an HB pencil, leaving none of the text unmarked, and as his ruler slid into angles and verticals, the pages turned into dazzling works, every one of them different. In the first row, almost under Wilton's nose, he bent industriously over his book, and the project of turning every printed page of Fowler & Smit into something new, was all the more exciting for being a secret act performed so publicly.

Fowler & Smit is of course garish, but it could be seen as Andrew Brown's first work of art, and as far as juvenilia goes, a significant pointer to Brown's mature iconoclasm. Drew laughs aloud at this foolishness that he dreams up in the name of Willem Stirling, the dreaded Cape Town art critic. He had once met Stirling at the National Gallery where he had just made the opening speech, and come to think of it, that was much like listening to old Wilton. These formal events are killers. At his own grand opening at Irma Stern, or why not the National Gallery itself, there will be no pompous speeches, no, it will be a Cape Flats *jol*, or else he, the artist, will refuse to attend. Not negotiable.

Jane keeps her distance from his world, but she worries when he larks about. They differ on whether it is healthy to fantasise. Ambition unhealthy? he queries, but she says no, it's a matter of indecency, this fantasising out loud. If he kept it under his hat as a dark brooding secret, he would keep slim, she says, and then she lunges at him under the covers, tries to grab handfuls of what she says are love handles. Which is of course not possible since there is not an ounce of spare flesh.

Drew is pleased with himself for combining the project he has in mind with their honeymoon. It could be said that the project has brought about the marriage and honeymoon, for how else would he have justified a trip to Glasgow? Janie was not keen on being married, why couldn't they carry on as they were, and she poked fun at the idea of a honeymoon. That's crap, she said; if it's a holiday let's call it that. Anyway it will be more of a *wittebroodsreis* than a honeymoon. That's all we'll be able to afford if we go to Scotland for our white-bread journey — pale, pre-sliced, flannelly white loaves from the supermarket with Bride's Pride in blue logotype on the plastic wrapping. They laughed at the translation, the paucity of down-to-earth, frugal Presbyterian pleasure. Let's not bother with marrying, Jane said, *wittebrood* doesn't go with a tiara. But, Drew said, Scotland, the home of Presbyterianism, is just the place to go for an authentic *wittebrood*. Imagine, you'll give them sutz *a skrik*, simmying in your Cape Flats bling like the Queen of Seba. Please think of Grace, he said, of how she can't hold her head up in Manenberg for the shame brought on her family by a layabout artist. So in the din of mockery and laughter she said yes, alright then, let's do it, at least marriage would please her mother.

That is how their own differences are resolved, the banding together against a world that seems to them sentimental, thoughtless, conventional, and one in which they flaunt their difference. Drew was over the moon. Yee-ha, he whooped, there was plenty of art he wanted to see in Scotland, and he also wouldn't mind doing a spot of work in Glasgow. And so the two things go hand in hand, which is another reason why his project must, for the moment at least, be kept secret.

Glasgow, as they both knew beforehand, is hardly the place for a Presbyterian *wittebrood*. Even bread is a designer item of many variations housed in what looks like exclusive bread boutiques; bling is to be found everywhere; and many a kirk has given up the holy ghost in order to become fashionable bar cafés. The opulence is awesome; their cents count for nothing, and they have to keep track of each paper-thin pound note. Which is why they've moved to a cheap hotel-cum-boarding house in the scruffier east end of the city.

Jane is irritated with herself for expecting Drew to behave as if they are on honeymoon. Even though the wedding was a hurried registry office affair in their everyday clothes with only her mother carrying an absurd posy of red roses and wearing a crazy hat, marriage has brought nothing but complication. If they were not married, she would certainly have expected them to do things together. Now, because it means nothing, because it is no more than a convenience, she must put up with Drew rushing about the place, leaving her to her own devices. It is as Jane thought: being a wife is rubbish, precisely because you have to be careful not to behave like a wife, or rather, not to be thought to behave like a wife. Which also sounds like rubbish ... Oh, it makes her head spin. She is sitting in an amazing space constructed from the backs of grand old buildings now enclosed, galleried, and domed into a modern square. The combination of old and new is piquant, and sitting in a cafe on the top gallery, she looks down onto the modern floor mosaic where a jazz pianist is absorbed in his playing, as if the place were not teeming with people.

Yesterday turned out to be expensive so that now she can only stare at the chocolate brownies, but there is a curious Presbyterian pleasure to be had from the deprivation, and the coffee will taste all the better. If Drew cannot be persuaded of the deliberate virtues of imposed daily rationing — he would rather run out of rands — she finds that being in control softens the blow.

Jane is as comfortable as can be. The music seems to encourage or at least legitimise loitering; after the coffee she will browse in the shops, so that I have no compunction leaving her in Princess Square. Besides, the rain has stopped and the glass cupola allows light to flood the place. Should she get bored, I could wheel in a juggler or a clown since the terraced space on the ground floor is large enough to accommodate a number of municipal activities laid on for the season of tourists and children's outings.

And so back to Drew whose story this is: he is forced into dissembling. He has in the last two days returned to the hotel to work on the book. It would have been so much better if the work had been done at home, but the truth is that until the very day they left, Drew was not sure what he would do. Now he puts up the Do Not Disturb sign and pays no attention to the cleaner who rattles the door in disbelief. Some monkey business going on here — she has after all seen with her own eyes the couple buttoning up their coats and leaving the place only an hour ago, but in deference to the sign does not use her key.

The book had been a green hardback without a dust jacket. Yesterday he scraped away at the embossed title on the cover before painting it red. The title on the spine is set into the fabric, with words arranged vertically, one by one: *The One that Got Away by Helen McCloy,* and at the bottom, the name of the publisher, *Gollancz.* Now painted, the letters are less clearly incised, barely readable. It is on the front cover that he works today with a stencil to print in large capitals an alternative title: GOLD MINING IN SOUTH AFRICA. Drew feels a momentary twinge of unease: what would Helen McCloy have thought of the alteration? He thinks of the author as dead, as indeed he thinks of all authors, who, if not actually dead, are ancient and chair-bound with long white beards. McCloy will of course not have a beard, or at least not a long one. He thinks of Aunt Trudie's, of the half-hearted migration from her thinning crown to the sparse crop of hair on her chin.

It is unease about the author that makes him flick through the pages, not for the first time, although he has no desire to read the book. His eyes are drawn to a word in italics. This is the hour we call *forenicht*, he reads, when you can see anything — ghosts of the dead and of the living, too, if you're a true Highlander. For a second he shudders at the thought of seeing the ghostly author with her wispy beard, but then takes comfort in the fact that he is not a Highlander. He fills in the new title with black paint; tomorrow he will alter the flyleaf and title-page. The book is placed carefully, open and face down, in his briefcase, which, before they go to sleep, he will unlock and leave slightly open for the drying of the paint. It is time for him to go; he has promised to meet Jane in Princess Square for tea at four.

But Jane is not there and her cellphone is switched off. Jane has been driven out by a pack of hungry-looking teenage girls, deathly pale in identical white sports outfits with hooded tops, who crowded round her. Leaning against the railing, facing her, they jeered in demotic that she could not understand, and as she bent down to secure her handbag, they split their sides, pointed and shouted, seeming to demand answers. But how was she to know what those questions were? The act of surreptitiously slipping her handbag into safety had to be recast as getting ready to pay the bill, so that she left for the safety of the till. The waiter thanked her effusively for the large tip, but he did not follow her out to the gallery where the jeering girls waited. Why on earth had she given a tip she couldn't afford? She stepped out briskly, running the gauntlet of girls, and shook them off as she made for the door. Outside it was pouring once again, and the girls did not follow her in the rain. Sugar lumps, she muttered gratefully.

The rain is by no means summerish; it does not fall gently like mercy from heaven. A vicious wind drives it in at an angle, so that Jane all but doubles up clutching her coat. She will go back to the room, to her bed, and snuggle down with a book. Drew will know where to find her.

The landlady, Mrs Buchanan, stops Jane on the landing. She is what is known as motherly, which is to say soft-spoken, kindly, full-bosomed, with rosy cheeks and fair hair fixed in the helmet style of middle-aged women of this town, no, of the world over. Jane notes her hair because she pats it compulsively, first with one hand, then with the other, and at times with both hands.

One or two days, the woman says, that's not a problem — and Jane wonders if she has just returned from an incident with her hairdresser, perhaps a new girl, an apprentice that she agreed to let loose on her hair, and now the regret — but tomorrow, the coiffured landlady hopes, her cleaner will have access to the room. Perhaps they could decide on a time that is convenient to both parties? And now both hands slap insistently like windscreen wipers at her temples.

Jane's look of incomprehension confuses the woman, who then remembers the cleaner muttering something about monkey business, so that she says she has just baked chocolate brownies, still warm they are, and wouldn't Jane join her for tea?

Her kitchen is nice and toasty, just the ticket for drying off with a nice cup of tea. Jane is ashamed of her anthropological interest in the woman's kitchen and hairdo, for having scorned the motherly look, since it is precisely what is known as motherliness that admits her into the warm sanctuary. Which brings a pang of homesickness for Grace's kitchen with its bubbling pot of soup, even though Grace is anything but, and in any case lacks the layer of plump that makes for motherliness. Puzzled as she is by the story about access and cleaning, she notes the detail of chocolate brownies, that which she had to forego in the cafe. The woman then is the counterpart of the jeering girls in tracksuits, and so Jane must not resist the pattern that presents itself, the story whose cast is growing, and which is sure to throw light on the darkness that is Drew's role, for it occurs to her as she bites into the sweetness of the chocolate brownie, that Drew must be up to something.

Drew had been researching the history of mining on the Rand for a collaborative art project with his pal, Stan-the-

Man. In the special collection of the Cape Town City Library he pulled out the dusty volume, and the novel literally fell off the shelf. He had not noticed it in the row of mining books. Perhaps it had been wedged behind the one he removed? Drew could not tell. The cloth binding was the exact green of the mining volumes, and the book was only slightly slimmer than the others. The title on the spine, *The One That Got Away,* suggested that it had nothing to do with mining, but fascinated with his find, Drew leafed through it. On the flyleaf was pasted the lending sheet of Glasgow City Libraries, and below, Dennistoun Public Library — Adult Department. The last date stamped in the final column of the lending sheet was 16 Jun 1976. Pasted onto the bottom of the gridded sheet was the standard information for lenders about the return and renewal of books.

Only later, after the meeting with Stan, did Drew wonder why he had, without thinking, tucked the book into his folder. It couldn't be called theft; perhaps it was to test whether the library alarm system would allow it, in other words, whether the book was a hoax of some kind. He did not think at all of why he had kept the find a secret. Immersed in the mining project, he gave little thought to the book, but kept it like pornography — from the Adult Department — under wrap in a manila envelope. It was a good two weeks before he had another look. He flicked through the book and gathered that it was a mystery set in the Scottish Highlands. Not his kind of thing, but it was the object and its history rather than the text that interested him. What would he do with it? He didn't know, but there was also the title that resonated, and the fiction that made him think of himself as a character whose role would become clear in time. He too, after all, was the one who got away, at least from the pin-stripe world of his brothers, the businessmen, the hollow men, the invisible men ...

Occasionally, he took the book out of the envelope and browsed through the pages. A mystery alright, although sections here and there appeared to be excursions into Scottish history and traditions. The faded pages were yellow around the edges, and Drew's nose twitched, as if foreign Highland spores trapped for decades between the pages leapt out to attack his sinuses. Thereafter he would turn the object this way and that, but try not to open the book.

Then came the business of marriage and honeymoon, or perhaps it was the other way round, since by then he knew with absolute clarity why he had taken the book. The last sentence on the library's lending sheet read: *A book must be returned to the library from which it was borrowed.* Such an injunction has to be taken seriously. It is the imperative, the indefinite article, and the mode of address that targets any reader, that at the same time orders him, Drew, to carry out the task. The text speaks to him: responsibility for returning the book does not remain with the one who borrowed it. Like any traveller then, the book will return, showing the scars of its journey, the markings of travel and adventure; it should return, flaunting its history and its difference. But how? That he didn't know until the very day of their arrival, so that he now has the task of transforming the object in a cheap boarding-house room.

Drew arrives at the cafe ten minutes late and Jane has gone. Her phone has been switched off, an infuriating habit that she cannot, will not be cured of. Just as she predicted, he knows that she has gone back to the room, knows that she has been driven back by the rain. He leaves a message for her — that he'll wander about for a while, that she should call him.

Mrs Buchanan's kitchen is unremarkable. There are the usual cupboards that hide mod cons like a refrigerator and who knows what else, as well as a large double stove. An Aga, she says, that is what she'd really like, just imagine, a warm kitchen with stockpot bubbling and loads of wee ovens to bake different things, over there a meringue in a cool oven, a casserole in another, and perhaps a nice loaf of bread in the hot oven here, all happening at the same time, and that, she says, is the beauty of it, the many things going on simultaneously, which surely must save time. Gesticulating, she loses the rhythm of patting her hair. Does Jane have an Aga? Jane has no idea what an Aga is. And what do people eat in South Africa? Jane has little interest in cooking, but she has a number of keywords at her fingertips and so does not disappoint Mrs Buchanan. *Biltong, bobotie, boerewors*, she recites, and then: *frikkadel, sosatie* — although she really has no idea what *sosatie* is. She passes on a tip that Drew's mother offered, the thing that makes Cape cooking so distinctive: a pinch of ground clove with all red-meat dishes. Mrs Buchanan says she'll try it, she's game for all kinds of culinary tricks, because if the truth be told, people here are fed up with bland food. Did Jane know that curry was now the favourite British dish?

The chocolate brownie is delicious. Jane eats two and out of politeness asks for the recipe. Then she spills her tea on the tartan tablecloth, but the woman says it doesn't matter. She giggles, It's a bit of a laugh isn't it, the tartan, but the tourist board recommends a bit of tartan here and there.

Before Jane goes she says, About the cleaning of the room ... But Mrs Buchanan brushes it aside. No need to worry dear; it really isn't a problem, and she pats her hair vigorously before adding that the forecast for tomorrow is dry and sunny, but cold, mind.

Jane does not consciously search the room, but she does wander in and out of the en-suite bathroom before settling into bed. What could Drew be up to? Again, if they were not married she could have grabbed him by the collar and shaken it out of him, but now she must be careful not to behave like a wife. She remembers the phone and calls Drew who is on his way back.

Ah, he sighs as he comes in, dripping with rain, just the ticket, just what honeymooners are supposed to do, and he whips off his clothes to snuggle into bed.

Jane recounts the events of her day, including tea with Mrs Buchanan, but says nothing of the room that has not been cleaned. A funny old thing hey, she says, this business of 'sharing' your life with someone. And she lifts her hands out of the covers to hook index fingers around the word. What is it good for? she asks, this telling of the things you did, the things that happened. Why do we do it? So the telling can tame the happening, the strangeness of experience, and ease it into the order of your shared life? Like writing the essay after reading the book: Discuss the role of chocolate brownies in Jane's day, she mocks. Perhaps if you were to keep it to yourself, undiluted, you'd deal quite differently with the dangers that breed in the day.

Drew looks into her eyes, smiling. He smooths back her hair. You're crackers, he says. Take it easy man, things happen, or we make things happen, and the talking is okay only if you feel like it. Listen, he yawns, there's a whole hour left before we get ready for dinner, please can we stop talking now, and hardly has he spoken before his breathing softens into sleep. When he wakes he says, You must have understood what the hooded girls were saying. No, she says, really, not a word. They just stopped in their tracks at the sight of me and started laughing and shouting.

Say *shibboleth*, he says, and she says, *Sibboleth*.

The next day it is Drew who suggests they do the Mackintosh architecture together. They visit the School of Art where she waits patiently while he examines the building in tiring detail. But at the Mackintosh House it is Jane who lingers, marvelling at the design of furniture and fabric and the simple magic of white gauze. That's it, she says, I'm going to take down those curtains in the flat; it's going to be all white gauze and diffused Cape light, and Drew laughs, Look who cares about decor all of a sudden. Jane has always deferred to him in such matters. Watch me, she says, I'm going shopping this afternoon with my credit card.

43

It is that afternoon that Drew finishes the alteration of the book. There are now two title pages: *The One That Got Away,* and another before it that reads in the same typeface: *Gold Mining on the Rand: 1886–1899 by Gavin Wilton.* He chuckles at the thought of old Wilton finding his name attached to a novel. With the book in a plastic bag, Drew goes to Dennistoun library on the next street, and has no difficulty slipping it into the fiction section between Wickham and Witworth. There are only two people in the reading room and they are stationed in front of computers. An attendant at the front desk is cleaning his nails. Drew nods briefly, formally, at the row of books and leaves. There is the satisfaction, but also the sense of loss that goes with finishing a project. Done, he says. He must have said it out loud, since one of the people at the computer looks up, and he leaves. The book has been returned to the library from which it was borrowed. Nothing major, Drew thinks, just a modest little project to go with a *wittebrood*. Before they go home he'll take Jane to the library; he will have to think of something to ensure that she takes the book from the shelf.

We sit in the twilight, the hour of *forenicht*, on the stoep looking out at Table Mountain on fire. Tonight's news says that a British tourist has set it alight with his cigarette. When the others go in to get drinks I ask Drew what he thinks. He fishes the typescript out of his bag and hands it over. I had imagined that he would keep it.

It's okay, he says, even if it's hardly a subject for a story. Really, it was just idle chat, just another event amongst things that happened on the honeymoon. He didn't think that someone would weave an elaborate story around it, hadn't imagined himself and Jane as characters in someone's story.

It is difficult not to be offended, difficult not to be defensive. Well, it's obviously not about you, or the two of you; it's just that I used your project — as one does, I add

44

lamely. I just thought you'd find it amusing to see what I came up with.

Yeh, it's okay, Drew repeats, shaking his head. *Ag,* I don't know, can't put my finger on it; I've always been rubbish with words. Perhaps it's the casting into words that seems to make a song and a dance about something that was not meant to be weighty. Now tamed further in the telling, as your Jane would say. All Chinese boxes hey, where will it all end?

There is a terrifying, cracking sound of fire, and a flare from the mountain lights both our faces.

Mrs Pringle's Bed

It is in the middle of the day, a mild summer's day for Cape Town, that Mrs Pringle wanders into the back room.

Annie peers at the thermometer fixed to the back door — a measly eighteen degrees Celsius. She totters into the yard with arms stretched out, trying to balance the full laundry basket on her head, for how else do you keep an interest in the washing, week after week, without setting yourself a challenge? Then, triumphant, if with a stiff neck, she is about to start pegging out when she sees the woman's shadow cross the lace curtain and remain perfectly still. So Annie stops to watch. *Aitsa*, this looks like trouble. She hasn't been in that back room for a while, hasn't bothered to sweep, not since old Pringle changed the bed herself, tossed the dirty linen into the passageway, and pulled shut the door.

There is nothing Mrs Pringle could claim to be looking for; she does not remember why she is there; her eyes sweep the clear surfaces of table and chest of drawers, then alight upon the bed, neatly made with tight hospital folds, and that is where they settle. Only two weeks ago Mrs Pringle herself produced these folds, so that the easy-care cotton cover turns the corners precisely at forty-five degree angles. Like the semi-transparent packaging folds around the curved corners of a sardine can which, as a child, a toddler really, she loved so passionately. Those she undid carefully; she wept when her mother tore impatiently at the paper. Brutal, that was the word that then came to mind, a word so apt that she wondered if she had made it up.

Why has Mrs Pringle, after Cousin Trudie's visit, not left the bed for Annie to change? And why, Annie wonders, has she not herself gone into the back room to check that things are as they should be, whether the embroidered cover is in place? Too late to worry about that now.

After standing perfectly still for some time at the foot of the bed, the woman moves as if in a trance. Through the lace curtain Annie sees with some difficulty the dim outline of raised arms, the silhouette that changes shape in slow deliberation as clothing is dragged this way and that, pulled over the head, as a knee lifts, a body bends, and then the figure is gone. A clumsy strip tease, and when the performance is over, it feels as if Mrs Pringle has gone for good. She might as well have been peering over a stack of suitcases, waving her hand from the window of a moving train.

Clouds skid hurriedly across the sky, across the window, wiping out the vision of a departed train. It is a day that could bring any kind of weather. Already it's so late to be pegging out the washing, but how is Annie to know that the day will be turning out so strangely? She sighs at the thought of what lies ahead: mud on the kitchen floor, damp washing, and Mr Pringle wanting his lilac shirt right away. He has lately taken to colour, ignoring the beautifully ironed white shirts he's worn all his life. Only yesterday she said to Mrs P: We must go buy some more coloured shirts, he don't like the white ones no more, but the old girl just stared at her rudely with those popping eyes, as if to say mind your own business, which would be fair enough if people didn't themselves drag her into their bladdy business. Yes, she too could be rude and say enough is enough, leave me out, but no she was brought up decently, so she lowered her head and said nothing.

Now there is whatever lies waiting for her in the spare room, although Annie hates to think of it as the spare room. It is her darling Daisie's, but she isn't allowed to call it that with Daisie married and away for over three years now. Mrs P says it is bad luck, that a married woman cleaves to her husband and that they should not be wishing Daisie to come home. Not that Annie thinks much of the idea of *cleaving*, a funny word that doesn't sound nice at all, and she certainly hopes that the child will come back if the *cleaving* turns out to be less than alright. She, Annie, has had her fair share of what they call *cleaving*, and frankly, nothing surprises her, but of course one can't speak of such things with the old girl whose head never tilts from that angle that Annie supposes to be an angle of correctness.

The door to the spare room is open. There lies the white cotton jersey on the floor if you please, all in a heap. The black nylon half-slip must have come off next. And against the lot, leaning stiffly, affronted, the bent permanent pleats of Mrs P's terylene skirt. Two shoes, the neat little black heels that the old girl wears even in the house, have been kicked off in different directions.

Must I bring Mrs Pringle a cup of tea? Annie asks the strange face, round as a moon on the pillow, but the woman appears not to see her. Perhaps there is a slight movement, a shaking of the head, and Annie backs out and shuts the door.

It is the 14th day of May, 1990, when Mrs Pringle takes to her bed. Daisie's bed, actually. She finds herself stripping down to her bra and *broekies*, slides carefully between the sheets, careful not to disturb the corner folds, and with her fingertips draws the cover up to her neck, lays her arms neatly by her side, and with no more than a shrug of the shoulders settles into a feather-soft, uncluttered world of rest. Her eyes shut with the click of the door — someone seems to be taking charge of things — and she sinks into dreamless sleep, the first in months and months of insomnia.

That must have been the trigger: the bare surfaces; the solid, tucked-in, coverless three-quarter bed, with no untidy drape or indeterminate hanging; the cupboard clear of all feminine clutter — a place where one can start afresh. There is no need to wonder why she has gone into the room. After a long life of hesitation and prevarication, Mrs Pringle has acted decisively, at last free of doubt. The sleep seems also to bring freedom from history. A smile of self-satisfaction plays briefly on her lips: to think that she herself has made this bed, prepared this clarity, as one would a room for a guest.

Cousin Trudie's visit has been too trying. That is the problem with a spare room, that other people will come and stay and poke their noses into one's business. Trudie is a talker, given to self-definition: one thing about me now, she would say, I just don't beat about the bush. And no sooner would that astonishing declaration settle than it would be followed by another hot volley of One thing about me ... It turns out that there are, in fact, many things about Cousin Trudie, although these have to be let out one at a time, lest the family be smothered by the richness of her qualities. She is shaped by an endless list of maxims disguised as personal attributes: she always looks trouble squarely in the face; never eats a cooked breakfast; knows how to give busybodies *min draad* (Mrs Pringle purses her lips at such vulgar language); never flinches in the face of adversity, yes, that too is now one more thing about her. Even personal preferences, like always taking butter rather than margarine, assumes the gravity of a moral choice, an essential aspect of her character that has to be announced. Cousin Trudie is keen on the idea of character: people are either characters or *gevrek*, by which Mrs Pringle understands herself to be without character. She will not use the other word.

On the third day of a visit that Mrs Pringle feared would never end — another thing about Cousin Trudie is that she always makes herself at home and never is any trouble to her hosts — Trudie lowered her voice to explain that she was not born a Pringle for nothing. They were of course an old respectable family from way back; she knew the Pringles inside out, and it was abundantly clear to her that Cousin Robert had strayed from the straight and narrow. In what respect she couldn't as yet say, but if the lilac shirt was not a sign she might as well give up. Mrs Pringle would have liked to ask what precisely she would give up, but the topic of lilac shirts was one she wished to bring to a close. Robert had not consulted her, had left the package for her to find, and then seemed surprised by his own purchases. By then, Mrs Pringle had long since stopped asking questions.

Cousin Trudie lowered her voice further to say that she, Polly Pringle, should put her foot down, that everyone knew that men over fifty went after floozies. Who would have thought that Cousin Trudie was capable of such language? She picked up her knitting and stopped listening. Polly Pringle ... Polly Pringle. She heard the chant above the click of knitting needles, in the clear voice of the young Polly weighing up the pros and cons of two eligible men. Then, at the age of twenty-three, an age her mother said was just right to be married, with two men vying for her attention, she chose Polly Pringle over Polly Kleintjies. Kleintjies sounded too much like the nickname of a farm labourer; it was no kind of name with which to navigate a respectable life. But it was not as easy as she publicly claimed. Herbert Kleintjies was a fine tall chap with wavy hair, and her heart lurched at his kind, soft-spoken manner. And above the sing-song of Cousin Trudie's maxims it didn't sound so ugly, or odd after all: her needles clicked to the moss-stitch rhythm of Polly Kleintjies. She knew of course that the world, or at least South Africa, had changed over the years, but how was she to know that things would take such an upside-down turn, that what passed for perspicacity then would sound pompous now? To Mrs Pringle's reformed, New South African ears, Polly Kleintjies had a clear ring of rootedness, of comfort, of straightforwardness that made her straighten her spine and spit out the lie: Daisie's husband phoned yesterday. He was going away and Daisie, being pregnant with a first child, did not want to stay on her own. She would come home, to her old room. Mrs

Pringle gave Trudie two days, then in a fit of generosity said no, that was a mistake — it was on Saturday that Daisie would come, an extra day's grace before she would have to leave. Although she trusted that Trudie would in the meantime mind her language and not use the F-word in her presence. Somehow, without thinking, she had dropped the honorific of Cousin. How old was Trudie anyway? She seemed younger than ever, plump with pomposity, a Pringle through and through.

Now Mrs Pringle lies in bed like any invalid with her arms neatly by her side. Later that afternoon, when she surfaces from sleep, Annie wheels in the glass-and-stainless-steel hostess trolley that she has been dying to use. On it is a pot of tea, a ham sandwich, and a freshly ironed nightdress which, on Annie's return to wheel back the trolley, Mrs Pringle is wearing, having tossed her underwear on the floor and straightened the bedclothes. She has eaten and drunk everything; she has after all missed lunch.

Would she like her knitting? Annie asks. Mrs Pringle looks blank for a moment.

Knitting? she repeats, as if she has never heard of such a thing, then, No, she says briskly, no — there is nothing left to knit; she's done it all, done with knitting.

And should Annie go ahead with *waterblommetjie* stew for dinner?

Oh yes, says Mrs Pringle, but Annie should in future consult with Mr Pringle. It may not always be necessary to cook dinner — as for herself, she isn't fussy, will pick at whatever is around.

Mr Pringle looks in before dinner. He leaves the *Argus*; he hopes that she will soon feel better. Mrs Pringle smiles sweetly and nods her thanks. She asks if he would be so kind as to remove from the white bedclothes a pink thread that Annie must have dropped. He stands helpless with raised hand, the thread pinched between his fingers, so that she suggests he take it to the kitchen. There's no bin in my room, she says. So it is done; she has said it herself: her room. When he makes to leave, without his customary clipped advice or even the most perfunctory of speeches, she tests the waters: yes, she is perfectly comfortable sitting up with the second pillow propped behind her, and the paper in the evenings would be very nice, thank you. She reads the *Argus* from cover to cover.

So Mr Pringle brings the paper every evening, and when he doesn't come home until late at night, he tiptoes with it into her room before going to work in the morning. Safeguarded against vexation, she takes up the weekend's *Mail & Guardian*, specifically saved for such evenings; somehow it just isn't right without a newspaper. Mr Pringle's original gesture of a raised hand with thread pinched between his fingers has transmuted into a girlish wave.

Annie hangs the candlewick dressing gown behind the door, and in the cupboard a few of the clothes Mrs Pringle has recently been wearing. Just in case Mrs P needs to get dressed in a hurry, she says, as if speaking to herself. And she gets away with it, with the abbreviation she would never before have dared say to the old girl's face.

Mrs P doesn't argue, although she can think of no reason for getting dressed at all, let alone in a hurry. She marvels at how free of vexation life has become since she came to bed. Who cares if Annie fails to Hoover and change the sheets on a Monday morning? She will presumably do these things on another day, and really there is no reason to fret. If Annie forgets that she does not like macaroni cheese, Mrs P eats it anyway, and finds to her surprise that really she doesn't mind.

And so Annie does her own testing of the waters. She deliberately does not wear the white regulation apron, brings coffee instead of tea in the morning, leaves the ironing until Friday, but her missus goes on smiling with other-worldly equanimity, so that Annie changes tactic once more and does her best to please. Indeed she goes out of her way: offers to run a bath every other morning for Mrs P; mends her nightdresses; washes the spare-room window. After lunch, she now awards herself a nap on the back stoep. It is only when the integrity of her room is threatened, a crumpled napkin or a spoon left on the bed cover, that Mrs Pringle minds. Then, if Annie is out of hearing, or snoozing, she is capable of getting out of bed with remarkable agility to straighten the covers or remove a speck of fluff herself before slipping back into bed. What a pity, she thinks, that Annie can't stay the night.

There are two worlds: one she encounters in newspapers, which occupies many a waking hour as she considers the editorials, takes sides on issues of local, national or international matters; and a second domestic world, of bedclothes and whatever goes on in the rest of the house, which is rapidly shrinking. At first, Daisie comes over and tries to coax her mother into getting dressed, but even the old pleasures of shopping have lost their appeal. Now Daisie sits by her bedside where they discuss politics, or the baby, for that is a subject Daisie cannot leave alone, but otherwise, Mrs P refuses to be drawn into discussions about people, or gossip, as she calls it.

Annie's taking advantage of your ... er, illness, Daisie says, but Mrs Pringle holds up her hand and shakes her head; she would hear nothing of Annie on whom she has come to rely.

Befok, that's what your mother is, says Daisie's husband Tom who hopes that the baby will not inherit any of her genes. For some reason Daisie repeats this but her mother smiles gaily; she is all for people choosing their own genes, but of course, nature sadly goes its own wilful way.

Sometimes, in the afternoon after their delicious naps, Annie would take tea with her. Annie also takes up the knitting that Mrs P has abandoned. The baby is due and surely the least a grandmother can do is to produce a moss-stitch matinée jacket. Which does not come easily, but Mrs Pringle advises and fixes dropped stitches. Annie is pleased with her new skill and buys complicated knitting patterns for the new baby.

Mr Pringle loses his bet. He assured Daisie that once the baby comes, her mother would be fine, would be restored to good health. Bet you five hundred rand, he said, when she raised an eyebrow. Mrs Pringle smiles healthily at the red-faced infant, expresses admiration for his neat Tom-inspired features, but offends them by not wanting its nappie changed on her bed.

My bed, Daisie snaps. They have all come to Mrs Pringle's room where the baby is being handed round and viewed. It now has become her space, she says, and smooths the covers of the contested terrain that she has awarded herself. Space? Daisie asks in disbelief, what do you mean 'space'? Her father is pacing before the window with his hands behind his back. Tom says that he hopes baby's pretty new ears will not be subjected to psycho-babble, and her mother nods serenely. It is Annie who saves the day. She has thought ahead. Now she darts out for the new padded plastic mat that will sit permanently on the table — it is only a matter of putting the news-paper on the floor, her eyes plead with Mrs P — where baby could be changed in comfort. Mr Pringle turns from the window to count from his wallet five hundred rand in ten crisp notes, which he hands to Daisie. He stoops to pinch baby's cheek and leaves with an extended version of the girlish wave.

It is Daisie who announces on Christmas Day that Annie will be leaving. Of course, Mrs Pringle says, she hasn't had a holiday in years, although it is her own fault. Since her mother has taken to bed, Daisie stays at her own home at Christmas and drops in briefly in the evening with a large plate of food, which Mrs Pringle wolfs down heartily. Mr Pringle has taken to holidaying somewhere out of town for the entire week.

I've said to her so many times that she ought to take her holidays. Imagine wanting to work every day except Christmas and New Year, says Mrs P between mouthfuls.

No, Daisie explains, it's husband troubles. She's got nowhere to go, except for family in Namaqualand. Her sister will have to find work for her there with white people.

Why has Annie not said anything? Is there a touch of glee in Daisie's voice?

Stop it, please stop it, Mrs Pringle shouts at her two-year-old grandson who is zooming around the room with the hostess trolley. He is making squealing sounds around imaginary corners as the trolley lurches on two wheels, so that Mrs P can't hear herself think. Daisie hugs the child, nursing his bruised feelings.

No need to shout Mummy, she says, gathering her things. And where exactly is Daddy holidaying? Shouldn't you know in case of an emergency, at least for his grandchild's sake? But Mrs P holds up her stop-sign hand and shakes her head. Her feelings are hurt. She cannot understand why Annie has not spoken to her. There is no question of the girl going away, what on earth would they do without her? Besides, she's not a spring chicken; she couldn't possibly start all over again with new people, white people to boot. With Daisie safely gone, Mrs Pringle allows fat tears to roll down her cheeks.

On Boxing Day, Annie arrives sporting vicious blue-black bruises on both arms. She tripped, she explains, carrying a pot of curried offal, and holding it up to rescue the food, bashed herself something awful. She demonstrates with her arms aloft and a deft skidding across the floor. Mrs P sends her to the bathroom cabinet for arnica, which she herself massages into Annie's plump arms. Mrs P's eyes are puffy with lack of sleep; she has been awake most of the night, thinking things through, but only now whilst tending to the woman, does a solution present itself.

So, she says briskly, *in medias res*, as she screws on the arnica lid, we'll start right away, by which she means that Annie will have to get going. Mr Pringle's study will have to be dismantled: his desk can go into the lounge which no one has used since Cousin Trudie's visit more than two years ago, and the bookcases should easily fit into his bedroom. She cannot remember what else is kept in the study, but Annie should use her own judgment on where to move things to, as long as the study is cleared. Annie is peeved. She may be strong as an ox, but she does not see her way clear to managing such a move, what with her bruised arms and all. And why should it be done now-now, and that on a Big Day? Does Mrs P not know that it's Boxing Day, a day for resting and snacking on luxuries? It's alright for those who do nothing but lie in bed all day long, but of course she does not say that out loud.

Nonsense, Mrs P says, carry the books through, and then you'll find the shelves quite easy to move. As for the desk, take your time. Take out the drawers, then take your time to push it slowly, carefully across the floor. Once it's in the lounge, just shut the door. Mr P can decide for himself how to arrange his things. According to his own taste and needs, she adds after a brief hesitation.

By the time Annie breaks off for tea and Christmas cake, she is covered in dust. The study has not been cleaned properly for some months, and no one has noticed. Perhaps old Pringle is punishing her today for the neglect, but as they drink tea together the old girl seems friendlier than ever, so that Annie suggests she finish the job the next day. Her arms ache with the carrying of dusty old books.

Oh no, says Mrs P, it won't do to leave things in that state. The lounge can wait, but the bedroom at least has to be restored to order. She has taken to calling it the master bedroom.

Before the end of the day, the study is empty and more or less clean, the curtains washed and pegged out on the line. Annie invites Mrs P to inspect the room, but the woman stares at her in astonishment. Of course she doesn't have the energy for that, besides, she explains, the room is now hers, Annie's, to do whatever she wishes, except of course have guests. It is up to her to inspect it. Tomorrow they will order a single bed, and Annie can select from the lounge any chair or table she might need. So no more nonsense talk about leaving, she finally explains.

Annie nods; she doesn't know what to think; she expects she'd get used to the idea. They drink more tea, and Mrs P asks her to take down the lace curtain, for the sun has turned blood red before ducking down, and now the window is on fire with orange and purple cloud licking like flames across the sky. Glory, glory hallelujah, Annie declares, but Mrs Pringle says it is best to savour the world in silence.

Mr Pringle arrives on the morning of January third, in time to change his clothes before setting off for the office. He explodes with rage, which frankly disappoints Mrs P. She expected better of him. She listens to him stomping about, banging doors and shouting at Annie — fuck this and fuck that and who the fuck does Annie think she is, moving into his room? She should get her fat Hotnot arse back to Bonteheuwel; does she think he wants to live like *Hotnos* with all types in his house?

Annie sobs loudly. Thank you very much, she says, she only carried out orders like any good servant, but she won't stay to take some people's insults. There is no way Mrs Pringle could enjoy her coffee with such shenanigans, such vulgar language, bouncing through the house. She calls sharply to Annie, makes her settle in the chair and have the coffee. After an ominous silence Mr Pringle announces loudly from the passage that he'll be back in the evening to collect his things. There is only so much humiliation a man can take, he shouts from the front door.

Annie packs his clothes and personal effects into suitcases, which in the evening are collected by a young man in blue overalls. The man will collect the rest of his things the following day.

Mr Pringle arrives with the *Argus* the next morning. He regrets that Mrs P will have to make other arrangements for the delivery of the paper; he does not see his way clear to performing that duty any longer. No doubt, he says bitterly, Annie will oblige. With his left hand he shades his eyes against the glare of the sunrise; he smiles wanly and gives a girlish wave as he backs out of the room. Mrs Pringle raises her arm to return the wave. When the door clicks shut, she eases herself out of bed, stretches her stiff arms, and from the cupboard selects a bright blue skirt and white shirt. Do these still fit her? She can hear Annie running her bath.

There's The Bird
That Never Flew

And who sculpted the water carriers? Or should she say modelled? That seems to be the word, at least back then, at the end of the nineteenth century, or so her leaflet on the Doulton Fountain says. Do they mean different things? But Jane will not pursue it. She has long since found a way out of such questions: I don't know anything about art, she would say, bowing out, and what's more, I don't even know what I like. Which never fails to amuse Drew. Come and give us your verdict Jane, he would say at exhibition openings and wait for her to deliver the line, upon which he would laugh uproariously. It embarrasses her. She doesn't know why she obliges.

Jane walks around the fountain once more. Can a monument be a work of art? Drew is not there to consult, although she suspects that he'd say it doesn't matter, that there is no need to decide. It turns out that questions are all that matters; no one seems to demand answers, and that is what she finds frustrating. No wonder coloured people don't care about art, she would mock.

You in love with an artist! her mother had screamed. Are you mad, after all I've spent on your education? How could you sink so low? Even overseas — I've seen it on the TV — they sit on the pavements or in city squares making pictures, and then people throw money at them. How would you like that Miss High-and-Mighty? So that's why he wants to go overseas hey, to draw on the pavements and hold out his cap where no one knows him?

But what if the cameras are there and the Isaacs next door just happened to turn on their TV? I may be nothing more than an old Griqua charlady but I have my pride.

Grace finds it puzzling, irritating, that her clever Janie, her late-lamb, should be so deferential, should claim that she doesn't understand what the man is on about. If she doesn't, then it is because it can only be — and Grace is sorry to have to use such bad language — plain old bullshit.

Fortunately for Jane, her mother's employer, Miss Haskins, is enthusiastic about artists. Special people? Grace repeated in disbelief, but Miss Haskins wanting to meet Drew went some way towards placating her. Except, Drew laughed and shook his head no-thanks, and so it was up to Grace to find excuses. Otherwise, she had to admit that he was pleasant enough, nothing like Tracy-Anne's layabout husband, although his people were hoity-toity, not her kind at all. More like *khoity-toity*, she said to Jane, no matter how toity, there's no getting away from the Hotnot, or Khoi, as you youngsters say these days, so with your B.A. you can just ignore their airs and graces. As for the neighbours, it was more convenient to say that her daughter was marrying a teacher, since how could they be expected to know that artists were special, that this one was not a beggar, planning to loaf his way about Europe. It was not as if they didn't all watch TV. And Drew had after all mumbled something about teaching. On being pressed, he said, pulling a face, that he could always teach if things got difficult. Drew! What kind of name was that? If his was the drawing business, then it was no good having a name that announced that his career was in the past, all finished and *klaar*.

Walking slowly around the railing of the monument, Jane smiles at Grace's indignation. She knows what her mother would say about these figures: not bad; why can't Drew do sensible things like this? Jane has by now formulated a number of questions about the figures, even if it is not a work of art, but she revises that — perhaps it's because it is not art that she is able to do so. Drew has disappeared into the People's Palace; he has cast only a cursory glance at the fountain. He chooses to believe that she is perfectly comfortable wandering about on her own, in spite of her disavowals, and Jane wishes she didn't care about not making sense of visual things. Her father, long since dead, may not have known much English but she remembers his use of the word 'uncultured', the pride of place it took on the rough edge of his tongue. For him, that was what placed people beyond the pale, so that he would shake his head disdainfully at the drunken brawl on the street, and declare them uncultured — they would never get out of Manenberg. Odd how the word still instills dread, even if he understood cultured simply to mean respectable, and somehow bound up with the incomplete set of *Encyclopedia Britannica* he had bought on the Parade. Odd to go on fearing an imprecation that turns out to mean something quite different from what she thought it meant. Jane wishes that she didn't care.

There is water in abundance — fountaining, spouting, or gushing from gargoyles. In shifting shapes, from clear arcs to extravagant spumes, in trickles or cascades, the water is white against the terracotta structure, bone white against the figures in marble. So even here, she notes, where it rains all the time, where water is commonplace, people are still diverted by such displays.

Jane had been waiting for the torrential rain to stop but, after nearly a whole day indoors, Drew, who had been rushing about the city like a demon after art, said it wouldn't do, that she really ought to get going. He waited impatiently as she tried on trousers, then a skirt, and finally settled for trousers. Jesus, it was supposed to be summer. She hated getting wet, hated the discomfort of damp clothes; she would rather read in the room and venture out if and when the weather improved. Drew said she was being silly. Should he not have greater regard for her feelings, her fear of fumbling with the unfamiliar, her hatred of being conspicuous, of being stared at, of shop assistants speaking slowly, loudly, to accommodate her foreignness, of children pointing? Who cares, he said, by then immersed in his notebook. She thought that he should. On her behalf.

Och, the woman cleaning the hotel lobby said in response to Jane's exaggerated shiver, it's a grand day, hen. She stopped, leaning on her mop, Yous don't want it too hot for doing the tourist things.

In Glasgow the familiar 'yous' was comforting. Just like Drew's Cape Town relatives, the aunties who had to be visited before the couple went on their overseas honeymoon. They sipped tea from cups that were introduced as if they were posh cousins with double-barrelled names. Royal Doulton Bone China, they were announced. And all the while the aunties offered advice: Yous must take your coats, even if it is summer over there; they say yous must watch out for the Cockneys, first-class *skelms*; and yous must stand your ground with the camera, those people *sommer* shove you out of the way with their camcorders. The aunties would want to see it all; they would throw a homecoming party for the photographs.

The new family-in-law certainly wanted to see everything. Aunt Trudie instructed Jane to kneel by her chair, and then unashamedly set about checking the hair in the nape of her neck for frizz. Always a give-away, the old hag said. Drew laughed uproariously, yes, she was absolutely right, it gave away everything about the one who investigates, but Aunt Trudie didn't seem to understand. Jane nodded stonily; she was outraged; she had expected more from Drew. Why was she unable to say anything? She went over the scene obsessively, trying out different lines, then settled for shaking the old girl up: Did Auntie Trudie not know that these modem chemicals were skin friendly, that the old nape test had become quite unreliable? So that the old woman smoothed her own thin strands nervously, checked that they hadn't retreated into frizz, and remembered that no one in her family cleaned for white people.

Well, a person can't take nothing for granted no more, what with the world all scrambled up and shrunk down by the computer things, Auntie Trudy complained. Unrebuked, unshaken, she urged them to be vigilant abroad. And she whispered chummily to Jane that she should take along some pantihose; they don't make them overseas in England. Her own daughter had come a cropper way back in the seventies. People didn't even know what she was talking about, asking for pantihose. So much for their overseas modernness.

Drew insists that there is nothing to it, nothing arcane about looking at art. It's just about giving it time, attention, looking carefully, because if you can describe a work accurately, you're more than halfway towards understanding what's going on. Easier said than done, but there's no harm in practising on the monument, even if it turns out not to be art.

The fountain is an extravagant memorial to Queen Victoria who is perched at the top. In the tier below her are classical female figures — water carriers. Jane remembers her mother's stories of the Griqua rain sisters, young women in starched *kappies* and large behinds who stumbled across the desert, sustained by *veldkos* and only the tiniest sips of brack water from their canvas flagons. The old people may not have had book learning, but they knew a thing or two, Grace would say, tapping her forehead; they knew that water leaks from the canvas and evaporates in the heat, so there you have it, ice-cold water in the desert, as if it came from a fridge.

That's the problem: Jane is so easily distracted; she promises herself to concentrate. The Queen's water carriers are in any case a far cry from the rain sisters. The four life-sized, elegant maidens vary only slightly in the curve of their torsos as they tilt pitchers of water over the colonial tableaux below. Really it is Queen Victoria at the apex who deserves a good dousing, if only to shatter that plump smugness. As if there had not been a warning against vainglory. The very weather had protested; in 1888, a bolt of lightning had struck that lady's newly-modelled head, killing her outright, and the City was right in wanting to replace her with an urn, but no, the Doultons, determined and drunk with the glory of Empire, had a second, imperious Queen Victoria made, and this time even the lightning desisted. Jane has done her homework on the extraordinary structure of the fountain. She has promised herself to make an effort to look at things without Drew's help; she hopes that effort is not inimical to the idea of looking. But can her views be trusted? And might he not say that if it's such an effort to look, then why bother?

The Doulton Fountain is a vast Victorian monument constructed for the 1888 International Exhibition in Glasgow's Kelvingrove Park. To celebrate imperial achievement, the information leaflet says. It does not speak of gold in the colony, of the rich Witwatersrand seams that lure settlers and investors, or of the war that looms. The fountain is circular; it accommodates arched niches for each of the colonies, and these house representative figures in terracotta, surrounded by typical flora and fauna.

Jane has walked around the fountain a number of times. The niches are much the same, and without the scrolls with the names of the colonies, they are indistinguishable. It starts raining again; she buttons up her raincoat; she will go in and find Drew. Will she remember all the tiers? Will she be able to describe the structure adequately? Jane glances once more in passing at the sheep and the beaver of Australia and Canada and the interchangeable human figures, and then on the east side, reaching South Africa, she stops as her eye glides from the quaint superscript below to the white head of the ostrich at the top of the niche. Of course, unmistakably the Cape rather than the riches of the Rand — the exotic flora and fauna that lured the Brits in pursuit of pure knowledge and scientific progress. No wonder the ostrich holds its head up for inspection. And then, following the line of the neck, Jane alights upon the woman she has passed over at least twice. How could she not have noticed before, for there in the niche, sitting cool as a cucumber in the Glasgow chill, is a young woman, no more than a girl, but unmistakably coloured. Jesus, she says aloud; she has not been looking properly after all, has missed the girl in all that elaborate Victorian detail and modelled in the same white stone as all the other figures.

South Africa, then, comes to offer a different kind of knowledge. Astonishing — and Jane stands transfixed as the water carriers seem to aim their pitchers at her — quite unbelievable that more than a hundred years ago, miscegenation was celebrated in a public work here in the 'centre'. She wonders if the figure was modelled from a real woman. She would have expected the burlesque of *Kaatje Kekkelbek*, whose author was after all a man from Thurso, or even a Saartjie Baartman who had titillated Europe with her spectacular behind. But no, the woman is exceptional only in her ordinariness. She sits in her niche, unembarrassed, demure as any woman of her time, and immune to the cold and the rain, presumably acclimatised by now.

The rain is bucketing down and the tableau is so blurred that Jane retreats to the Winter Garden. She sips slowly at the carrot-and-coriander soup, trying to make it last, for once it is finished she will not know how to remain comfortably at the table. Drew breezes in; he is in a rush, there is another place he could take in if they leave immediately. Jane does not catch the name, but no, she doesn't want to go; she'll stay a while and see him back at the hotel. She watches with amazement as Drew grabs the bread roll left on her plate, takes a bite, and walks off with a wave of the hand holding the half-eaten roll. She marvels at his lack of self-consciousness, at his not caring what the waitress might think, although that, of course, is about being a man. But it gives her courage:

she will stay there out of the rain for a while. Jane takes out her notebook and pen and orders another cup of tea.

What was it about the ostrich that left Mr Ellis, artist and modeller in stoneware and terracotta (c.1877-c.1910), head over heels in love with the creature? It is true that he had bought Mrs Ellis an ostrich-feather boa, which he wrapped around his lady's throat, and that that lady used it shamelessly to wrap him around her little finger. But there was so much more to the ostrich. It was no accident that Ellis landed the commission for the South African niche. Gifts had been sent to Doulton, emissaries chosen to importune on his behalf, but only when he finally pleaded the importance of the ostrich, no less significant than the glittering new diamonds, was he given the commission. At last he would create a life-size ostrich, magnificent with its curved neck, its head held proudly aloft, and all the more alluring for being half-hidden behind the human figures. But the girl brushing against the sinuous neck and the fulsome plumage would feel its feathered glory. Ellis has failed to persuade his missus to emigrate, and so he must forego adventure, the call of the wild, and stick to modelling, for the truth is that he will never produce art. Mrs Ellis consoles. It's all rubbish, she says, emperor's clothes and all that; none of those fashionable artists have your skill, and she buys him books on the colony. He has read Mr Pringle's narrative, his travels through the Karoo with the account of the ostrich that corrects the popular view of the creature's stupidity. A long description of its nesting habits shows the sagacity of the bird, so that Ellis's own model shows a visage infused with intelligence, a bird fitting for the beauty of the girl. He has tried to read Geddes Bain, a fine road engineer indeed, but the man should have stuck to roads. Ellis can't or perhaps won't read his *Kaatje Kekkelbek*, written as it is in the vulgar dialect of the girl herself, and in any case he believes the poem also to be an insult to England.

The next day, Jane returns to the fountain whilst Drew again charges about the city. It promises to be dry, and she ought to have another look, for what else might she have missed in the blur of rain? In the foyer, as she sets off, she meets the cleaner, who asks where they are from. The woman is delighted. Ah Nelson Mandela, she says, he's a real man, never mind the nonsense people talk about him being a saint. She wouldn't mind tangoing with him — the old men are best, more appreciative of a woman. Her Highland people went out to South Africa a good two hundred years ago when the country was brand new. And like everything in God's world that is dressed up to be all the rage, they should have known that it would end in tears. A fricking disaster it was too: imagine the horror of fire raging on a ship in spite of water all around, mocking them, so that most were burnt to a cinder, wee flakes of ash — and the woman pinches with her thumb the tip of the index finger to show the size of flakes — blown overboard well before they were even in sight of the promised land. Which meant that her own great-great-grandfather, waiting at the dock for the next ship, went home to unpack his trunk and stay put. Now she understands that the handful who survived are stinking rich, swimming pools and such, but mind, she says nodding sagely, there's nought for nothing, a price for everything if you asked her. The woman is called Margaret, but Jane doesn't know her name, is too embarrassed to ask so late in the day.

Jane asks what she thinks of the Doulton Fountain. Margaret hasn't seen it; it's only been moved there recently, although she seems to remember it elsewhere on the Green, carted over from the West End they said. She was only a girl then, but she recalls the monument being a dump, all in a mess, the fountain dead, statues without noses, the Queen's head lopped off as the winos threw their bottles of Buckfast at the figures, and the dogs shat in the dry moat. She, Margaret, doesn't give a toss for all them tourist walkabouts. She nods at Jane with friendly contempt. See yous, she says cryptically, yous get to see everything, but yous dinnae know a thing about the real Glasgow. That's why she stays put like that great grandda, stops at home, best place from which to keep an eye on the world. The woman pronounces the word like a Xhosa-speaker, inserting another vowel so that it sounds almost like the Afrikaans 'wêreld'. Jane thinks she might be referring to the ease of the internet; she nods sympathetically. If it were not for Drew, she too would stay put, she says. But Margaret wants to get on with her own story, another family history about fires.

See that building across the way from the fountain, the Templeton carpet factory copied from some fancy place in Italy, she isn't sure where, well, that was the site of another disaster where her own grandmother died. They may go overboard on the Health and Safety these days, but in them days ... Margaret snorts derisively. So busy were they making the grand façade, making money out of working folk, that they clean forgot about Health and Safety, and a blazing fire broke out in the factory killing so many weavers. Another tourist attraction now, but did Jane think that was a place she, Margaret, wanted to ooh and ah about? Then she whips out a packet of photographs from the pocket of her overalls. See here, she says, my son and the new grandchild, and Jane dutifully ooh-ahs about them. She hopes they'll survive the fires of Glasgow. Staring intently at the close-up of the baby with its swollen red cheeks, it strikes her that she would not like to have a baby. To reproduce a fearful, tottering creature like herself, brimful with embarrassment, cannot be a good thing.

Jane wanders about the fountain, taking in the uniformity of the figures, the commonalities of the tableaux. No wonder she failed to note the difference in South Africa. Doulton's designer must have had a limited number of features. Take your pick, he would have said to the sculptors, the trick lies in repetitions, so that even the Indians, in spite of the man's turban, seem to be modelled on the same white people. And heavens, she is disappointed in herself for not having looked carefully, for she has also missed the difference in the Australians. Here the arrangement is reversed: it is the man who is seated, his left hand leaning on the haft of a spade. The Australian woman stands tall with wheat sheaf clutched in her left hand, the other resting on the curved horn of the sheep. In all the niches are couples, future mummies and daddies with agricultural produce that presage babies. The men are mustachioed. The women are bearers of bounty. Clustered around their figures are the ears of grain tied into sheaves and cascades of grapes. Bucolic, like harvest-festival displays, and not a gold bullion in sight.

Jane fingers her ring of plain white gold nervously. After all these days, the eighth to be precise — they had spent several in London — it still feels strange. The tip of her finger is almost white, as if the flow of blood is restricted. If it were not for Drew, she wouldn't bother to wear the ring, which draws attention to her knobbly fingers; indeed, she is banking on him losing interest in it. He had after all happily given up the idea of wearing one himself when she said she didn't care. Why then does he think she should wear a ring?

Just as Jane squats to make notes on the South African woman who, like the Canadian and Indian women, is seated, the rain starts sifting down again. She will have to put up with it. The choice here is between ignoring rain or spending a fortune on cups of tea indoors. Kaatje, that is what she'll call the woman, never mind that with her quiet confidence she couldn't be more different from Baines's crass *Kaatje Kekkelbek*. She is conspicuously native. Not only are her facial features — cheekbones, nose, full lips — distinctly Khoi, but the fullness of hair framing her face speaks unashamedly of miscegenation. It is the plumage of the ostrich that is repeated, refashioned in that crown of tight curls. To her left is the bearded white man, a boer with bandolier across his shoulder. His right hand rests on the row of cartridges that cover his heart, and under his left arm the butt of a musket that drops to the ground. He wears the boots and broad-rimmed hat of the frontier farmer. Beside him Kaatje's left arm is crooked, so that her hand rests on the haft of a spade that leans somewhat towards her. To her right are the symbols of fecundity: grapes, luxuriant foliage, and her hand narrowly escapes a cascade of water from the urn above. Centred above her head is that of the ostrich perched on phallic neck. Its feathers fill the space between the two figures.

Unlike the man, the seated Kaatje is unshod. Does that mean she's a servant, that the farmer has been sculpted with his *meid*? The two figures looking out of the tableau do not instantly reveal their relationship to each other, but the fabric of the woman's classical garb brushes against his right leg, partially covering his knee, which is turned out slightly towards her. The brush of clothing and the symmetries, the repeated verticals of spade and rifle in contact with each left hand, are metonymies of matter-of-fact intimacy. They are unmistakably a couple.

Kaatje's posture and facial expression tell that she is not a servant; she occupies her space with ease, not regally like Victoria, for she feels no need to claim space, no need to assume an imperious pose. Her limbs under the inappropriate, rigid attire are relaxed, feet planted firmly on the ground, as if savouring a rest from toil. Her slanted Khoisan eyes gaze out brightly at the world, with neither arrogance nor humility, rather, with calm curiosity as if she knows of her transportation to the metropolis and does not mind at all. Her difference is not a burden, and hence the astounding paradox of a sculpted figure who will not be an image; she cannot be subjected to anyone's gaze. No wonder Jane had missed seeing her. Whilst her descendants at the Cape have been either cringing with shame or living up to the Kekkelbek portrait, Kaatje has been sitting here bathed in grace for more than a century, unembarrassed. As for Aunt Trudie:

Kaatje would not mind the old bird at all, would lean her head into that bony lap, luxuriate in the probing fingers, and click her tongue soothingly at the foolish woman.

Drew, enjoying an overpriced dinner in the Merchant City (in the process of regeneration, he reads), falls head over heels in love with the woman he has married. She is explaining to him, the minutiae of the monument, of how Kaatje Kekkelbek — Jane is sure that the woman doesn't mind the name at all — sits nonchalant in her niche. Jane is ravishing in red. Her eyes flash, and she waves her arms and hands by way of demonstrating. Has she had more than usual to drink? They walk back to the hotel in the rain, her head leaning on his shoulder.

It is in the bath the next morning that she finds her ring gone. She remembers rubbing it whilst looking at the colonial couples; in any case, she has not once taken it off since their marriage. Margaret whom she asks to look out for the ring, winks at her and says earnestly that she shouldn't worry. St Mungo, the patron saint of Glasgow, will keep an eye. Did Jane not know the Glasgow legend? Margaret recites:

There's the tree that never grew
There's the bird that never flew
There's the fish that never swam
There's the bell that never rang.

Look, she says, grabbing from the pile in the foyer a brochure with a picture of the City's coat of arms, the fish carries a ring in its mouth; it's fished it out of the fountain.

Later, when Jane recites the rhyme to Drew, he says that his granny used to sing a similar song, about a chicken, and a horse, he thinks, where each line, in the form of a riddle, is repeated before the answer is given. He sings lustily, repeating all three lines, and hums through the words that escape him.

Daar's 'n hoender wat 'n eier nie kan lê nie
Daar's 'n hoender wat 'n eier nie kan lê nie

73

Daar's 'n hoender wat 'n eier nie kan lê nie
En dis die haan wat op die kerk se toring staan ...
Daar's 'n perd wat hmm hmm nie kan hmm nie
En dis die perd wat op die whisky-bottel staan.

Drew says it must be modelled on St Mungo's unsung ditty. He is doodling on his pad, idly sketching the lines of a church tower with weather vane where he will perch a cockerel with a ring on its toe. And he laughs. See how the Glasgow story seems to regret the difference between the real and the image, whereas our colonial version is upbeat, ready to celebrate representation, or one could say that the real ... But Jane stops him. Could he not, for once, listen to her? She has lost her ring for heaven's sake; she doesn't know what to do, and no fricking fish is likely to dart from the fountain with her ring in its mouth.

Fricking fish! Fricking? Drew laughs. Look, it's only a ring, and it may well turn up, but if it doesn't, who cares. You don't even like wearing it. Bet your Kaatje doesn't wear a ring.

It is true. Kaatje doesn't wear a ring. Or, Jane revises, frowning in concentration, the woman's left hand clutching the spade — damn, for all her looking, she can't be sure. But Kaatje wouldn't care, would not deliberately keep her finger hidden. Kaatje doesn't give a toss, as the character, whose name Jane doesn't know, would say.

Neighbours

They have moved into a nice house of their own, Jeff'n' Marie, in a nice old terrace built by the Church of Scotland way back in the 1800s. A solid house with foundations of granite, and across the way, cute squirrels scurry up and down huge old trees on the green. Which — with houses on only one side of the streets overlooking the green, or rather the private gardens — surely makes it a Square, although the space is, strictly speaking, a rectangle. Such a pity then that it is named Bilsland Street rather than Bilsland Square.

Och nevermind, Jeff consoles, it's the experience of living on a private square that counts, rather than a posh postal address, and so, with a comforting G'n'T, for it is luckily a Wednesday evening, the matter is put to rest. Jeff'n'Marie have since their retirement settled for a pre-prandial G'n'T on alternate nights; however, the inconvenience of a week having seven days means that both Friday and Saturday are drinking days but then, jolly hollies, that's what weekends are all about, and besides, it fixes a pattern of Monday and Wednesday as the nights for a wee dram. (Which is what they call it, although when offered a whisky, they shake their heads decisively: we're G'n'T people.) Who knows, Jeff jokes, that we wouldn't otherwise lose track as the old Alzheimer's sets in. Which is of course nonsense, and he relies on Marie to protest that no one has a healthier, stronger constitution than he.

The children are gone, fled the nest, Marie says across the fence to the new neighbour, a single parent it seems, whose grown-up son lives there, no doubt sponging off his mother. There is a satisfying finality about the words, so she repeats: aye, fled the nest — relishing the sound, and not as the neighbour woman must think, out of smugness. Marie is not insensitive to the cloud that scuttles across the woman's face before she rearranges her expression, what with being a single parent she must be practised in putting on a good face. Ben, that's her name, so it's not surprising she couldn't remember it right away. There is a light knock from the window where Jeff keeps half an eye on Marie, but she pays no attention. She still hasn't got round to the unpleasant task of telling Ben that the weeds in her front garden won't do, that the west wind that funnels down this street spreads the seeds before you can say flibbertygib. Of course she won't mention the junk in the back garden, for that would be tantamount to saying that from their bedroom window they're keeping an eye on her. At least not yet, since Ben has only just moved in, but sooner or later it will have to be raised otherwise there'll be an invasion of rats.

If only Marie could remember the son's name she could say how he no doubt will be tackling the weeds. She supposes the lad to be the woman's son, although Ben is no spring chicken. She could add that it took them, Jeff'n' Marie, ages to get their garden into shape.

Marie settles on sympathy. It's a shame, she says, that the garden had been so neglected — as if there's not enough to do getting a new place in order. Moving house certainly takes it out of you, and of course in all the time it was left empty the weeds went wild in the sunshine. But I expect that strong lad of yours will soon put it to rights. If it's a hoe the lad wants, him indoors will let you have one, and also, we've got stuff left over for treating the lawn that you're more than welcome to. Eradicates moss in a matter of days, she quotes from the packet. The damp's the devil for spreading moss, and then it chokes out the grass. But weeds, they won't let anything choke them; there's no getting out of hard graft, and what with summer on its way, there'll be a riot of weeds. But your lad is welcome to borrow anything he needs.

If the woman has any sense she'll know that this applies to the back garden as well, will infer that the junk is offensive and will have to be removed shortly. It's not as if the Council doesn't help, but then the woman probably doesn't know, being foreign and all. Marie wonders why she has mentioned Jeff; it is after all she, Marie, who has taken on the lawn.

Ben does not look grateful at all; indeed, she raised an eyebrow at the mention of summer heat. She smiles serenely and says that she has nothing against moss, that there is no point having expectations of Rube, that she too appreciates a nice garden, but then, weeds are not the end of the world. Has Marie noticed how wonderful the dandelion looks this year? One can't imagine how they came to be classified as weeds, especially with the leaves being so good in salad as well.

Marie is speechless. She looks pleadingly at the window but Jeff, having given up on her, is engrossed in the newspaper. Her eyes dart up and down the woman's faded T-shirt and jogging trousers rolled up to the knee, until the words come in hardly more than a whisper, sorrowfully, Oh well, there-there then, as if comforting herself, before turning to go.

Ben is a nurse. She is concerned that the woman, whose florid colour has deepened to an alarming purple and whose eyes seem to pop, is clearly not well. Most probably a dickie heart.

Jeff is reading *The Scotsman* as he does on Saturday mornings in Dad's chair in the lounge. Marie demands that he put the paper down. Imagine, she pants, not the end of the world! What kind of low-down thing is that to believe, never mind say out loud. It's disgraceful, wherever you might live, but in a street like this ...

Jeff stops her with an impatient yeh, yeh.

There is no need to say it out loud — that having been careful with money all their lives, having scrimped and saved, they do not deserve this; that it is disappointing to find themselves with a neighbour who fails to appreciate that the street is in fact a desirable square. The woman's views are themselves like weeds that will multiply wantonly and invade the artful order of herbaceous borders; they cannot be tolerated in Bilsland Street.

Marie's fury is directed at herself. It is self-evident that moss in a lawn should be thoroughly sprayed and raked out, otherwise it could not be called a lawn, and she should have had the courage to explain that it's all change here. It may have been a run-down area once, but it's been respectable for a while now, and with the fine homes renovated, the prices are soaring, and not every Tom, Dick and Harry ...

Jeff says irritatingly that the woman with a bloke's name must know that; she has after all just paid a fortune for her house, though you have to wonder how such people could afford it. What Marie ought to have pointed out is that standards have to be maintained, that it is every home-owner's responsibility to do his bit, a matter of common decency.

Well then Dad, she says tartly, it's up to you to let her know.

Jeff is a man of action. Right you are, he says and rises with a little grunt. His knees are not what they were; how much longer would he have to wait for the fricking National Health to come up with a replacement? From the coat rack at the front door he takes the tie and jacket kept there for emergencies, and in the process of dressing comes up with a plan. He collects the hoe and the half-full packet of Lawn Care from the shed, and straightening his shoulders sets out, careful not to limp. At the neighbour's door he puts down his equipment and, ignoring the silly cutie-cat door clanger, knocks forcefully.

When Ben opens the door she staggers back as his right arm shoots out, surely to punch her in the face, but he bellows in a military voice — something about a hankie? Sorry? she stammers. What on earth could the man mean?

Shankie, Jeff Shankie, he repeats, then more slowly as he notes her frown: Number fifty-two, and she understands that the hand is being held out to be shaken. His eyes rest for a second on her breasts lolling freely under a T-shirt. Look, he says, stooping to pick up the stuff, I've brought a hoe and a packet of Lawn Care. It's quite simple. If your lad's about, I'll show him what to do.

Ben turns and shouts up into the stairwell. Rube, are you up? Then louder: Rube, Rube.

A muffled voice replies, Fucking hell, its only just eleven, go away, leave me alone, and then a final drawn-out Fu-uck!

She smiles fondly. Looks like you'll have to do the gardening without Rube. At weekends he doesn't get up until midday. I suppose he's spoilt; you know how it is when a late-lamb comes along, when you've forgotten how to raise children. If it were not for the cupboard I'm painting, I'd happily give you a hand.

Now look here Missus er ... But she interrupts, holding up her ringless finger: Ben, please call me Ben.

Right you are, Ben, but it won't do, you know, no it won't do; it's a matter of discipline ...

Again the woman interrupts. Oh, and how's your wife, I meant to ask, she didn't look at all well.

Jeff's colour rises. He's no fool; he has a nose for cheekiness, and that he will not tolerate; he must keep cool. The wife's fine, he says briskly, now let's get down to business, get this garden of yours sorted. As soon as your lad stirs hisself — and he stumbles for a second, revising — as soon as he stirs himself, he's got to start at the weeds with the hoe. Then it's a matter of scattering the Lawn Care evenly across the grass and two weeks later you rake out the dead moss and remaining weeds. As simple as that. Your boy can knock on my door for a rake if you don't have one.

Ben decides not to argue. These people are excitable: the man looks as ill as his wife, and she had better let him be. So she smiles, thanks him, and shows the old geezer to the door. Ben supposes that this exhausting business is what's called neighbourliness; she had always wondered why such a category should exist, how it could be different from just being a decent human being who would readily lend a hand or a cup of sugar. Now she understands the underlying concerns of ownership, the need for uniformity that neighbourliness must police.

Marie's what-happened questions are irritating. Jeff gives a short edited version. But she wants to know what the house is like, a question he really can't answer because that's not what he went over for. Marie knows that information will come slowly, will slip out apropos of nothing at all over the next week or so. But why is he wearing his tie? It's Saturday morning for heaven's sakes, and he has plenty Saturday-morning casual wear. She helps him off with the tie.

It is still a couple of hours to lunch and Marie is at a loose end. No question of going back into the garden, even if there is so much to do. What if the woman were to come out and lob more unpleasantness at her? Newspapers bore her, especially the kind that Jeff has taken to reading since they moved here, and anyway, she'd not be reading *The Scotsman,* would she? Besides, Jeff usually reads out the titbits that he knows she'd like to hear. The solution is to start preparing lunch, and with the extra time on her hands it might as well be something fancy. They are both partial to lasagne and if that is a bit extravagant for lunch, what the hell, after this morning's bombshell they deserve a treat. On Saturday afternoons, they have a nap or rather, they often have private activity, followed by a nap. Ever since the children were small and went off to play and later went to the shops, she has turned on the little television in the bedroom and received Jeff's measured pumping to the ups and downs of *Coronation Street* folk, who she must say, are coping with all sorts of interesting, fashionable predicaments. Time was when you expected ordinary folk to have common ways, but nowadays there's little to choose between ordinary and gentlefolk, although there'll always be the riff-raff types who let the side down. Jeff'n' Marie had even thought of retiring to a nice little village, but in the end neither of them was keen, what with being born and bred here in the city.

Just as well she has watched this episode earlier in the week, since, with a limited view of the screen, Marie doubts that she'd make any sense of these shenanigans in *Coronation Street*. Today, Mrs Thingummy's argument about frozen embryos, which she doesn't mind hearing a second time, is interrupted by Jeff's hushed shudder and sigh, and as he rolls off, burying his face in the pillow, he asks if she thinks the neighbours are British, if she's seen the boy.

Marie says of course not. The woman is quite dark, quite different, and the boy, if she's not mistaken, is even darker. On the other hand, it takes all sorts these days. The woman's saving grace is that she does speak nicely, not your common type.

Jeff lets out a bitter laugh. Not common! We should be so lucky. You should've heard the boy's effing and blinding from his bedroom, and at his mother as well.

Marie is devastated. There is a loud pounding in her ears, and her eyes drift to the dividing wall where she imagines the woman to be sitting, trying to listen, and practising her swearwords like the French verbs you had to learn at school. It is best to keep her thoughts to herself, no point in upsetting Jeff, but really this is not good at all. The problem with bad language is that bad deeds are sure to follow. They will just have to be vigilant, and now that she imagines the woman on the other side of the wall, she doesn't know whether the Saturday-afternoon activity won't have to be put to rest. She'll have to think of something else for Jeff to do.

Later in the early evening as Jeff 'n'Marie settle down to their G'n'Ts, loud music starts up next door, but just as they get anxious, going through the options of how to deal with it, the music is turned down. Marie's warning that they should take it easy, not give the neighbours the power to upset them, especially since the sound is now easily drowned by their own television, is really a warning to herself. But Jeff spoils it all by saying that since the houses are not made of glass the neighbours have no way of knowing whether they are riled or not. What worries him is that the day has gone by and that idle yob next door has done nothing in the garden.

Fortnightly, on Sundays, Jeff'n'Marie visit Aunt Sally in the old folks' home. They take biscuits and Thornton's cut-price misshapen chocolates, which are of course as good as the well-formed ones in fancy boxes. Besides, Aunt Sally stuffs handfuls into her mouth; she is not good at chewing. Her sunken cheeks plump up with half-chewed sweets that dribble onto an already dirty pinafore and often land down the side of her chair, but the old woman won't allow Marie to mop it up. She is ninety-three and therefore is forgiven, just as her high-pitched ramblings are treated with the credulity they do not deserve.

Even on a Sunday, the old woman complains, these workmen with their pneumatic drills are hard at it. Enough to drive you crazy any time, but on the day God's given us to rest — it's terrible. I've got a good mind to go out there and give them what for. Marie tries to calm her down.

There's no one out there today, Aunty, no machines, just the little birds singing their hearts out, she soothes.

But the old woman is indignant. Don't be daft. Look, there are workmen milling about that huge machine. See the yellow one, it's a digger with great big claws, and screwing up her bat-blind eyes she leans forward to read from an imaginary machine: B — A — B, yes, she says triumphantly, it's written on the side there in black letters, B-A-B-Y-L-O-N Constructions. And the men, effing and blinding like there's no tomorrow. Well, there won't be, the way they're going on. And all the while struggling with the chocolate packed into her mouth. Marie has surreptitiously slipped the packet under the bed-cover. Aunty won't remember if they're out of sight, and when she finds the packet later, well then, she can scoff the chocolates and dribble as she pleases.

Och, it's a wee job, trimming the hedge. The men'll be packing up soon; they're just about done, Marie plays along.

Jeff is embarrassed, not only by the old woman's hallucinations, but also by Marie's foolishness. Aunt Sally is his father's sister and he can only hope that he hasn't inherited the mad genes; he certainly will not be going into a nursing home where for all its tidiness and nice gardens the smell of shit hovers just beneath the disinfectant. Mind you, without the old girl's hallucinations it would be hard to fill the statutory forty-five minutes they set aside for the visit.

Nice and bright she looks, Marie says as they leave, and Jeff shoots her a quizzical look. Is she too going mad? Perhaps it's a female thing. His father after all was in sound mind when he died at the respectable age of seventy-eight with both knees in good working order. No need to live beyond seventy-eight. That is certainly when Jeff plans to go. No Methusalah madness for him. He understands that the Scandos sell a suppository over the counter, even at their corner shops, to bring things to a tidy close, and that's just what he'll be doing. At some point he'll take Marie over there, to the north; fingers crossed she'll see the sense in it. Nothing morbid about that. It's a matter of good sense, of thinking ahead, just as he had to think ahead with a nest egg for their retirement, and a fine job he made of those investments. G'n'T night would be suitable for such business, and then they could allow themselves a double, actually, come to think of it, as many doubles as they can manage, although that might make things messy. It has to be a neat affair — there are the children to consider. Jeff does not like to think of administering the suppository. Marie is good at that sort of thing — she has a First Aid certificate, and he must agree that she is good with Aunty. Happily there is no need as yet to think about such matters; they are both in good health, and even if he says so himself, they look remarkably well for their age.

Mum, he says in a rush of affection and under the crunch of wheels as they pull up in Bilsland Road, why don't you put your feet up this evening, and I'll do a barbecue. It's going to be a smashing evening, so we'll sit out in the back garden. Good thing it's a G'n'T night. Marie pats his hand. She is a lucky woman; for all his foibles, he is a good husband; he cares well for her.

They are about to open the gate when loud chatter and laughter from the green across the way stop them in their tracks. It is difficult to see at this time of year when all the foliage is out, but surely behind the redcurrant bush something is going on, something inconceivable so that, for a second, Jeff is distracted by the bush itself. He had hoped to get it cut down and replaced by a nice holly; he hates the cat-piss stink it bellows out all through the summer months, but the old girl at the top of the road objected. She loves the currant bush. It smells of incense, reminds her of church, she says.

Their eyes follow the flashes of colour — women's clothing? — that appear between dense branches. Shadows flit to and fro behind the bush, surely figures moving about, and also laughter. It is unthinkable that a group of people should be carousing in the communal gardens. Jeff is chair of the local residents' association, indeed, he is the founder, and damn it, it's there in the constitution, a motion proposed by him and passed unanimously, well, with no protest to speak of: There shall be no picnicking or gathering of any kind in the private gardens. Typical of folk, waiting for someone like him to come along and set in print, in stone, their heart's desire.

Jeff straightens his tie and storms to the gate, which opens without the help of the key that he tries to find on his ring. The ease with which the unlocked gate swings back makes his heart stop for a second; something at the core of his stomach has been wrenched open, floodgates, and a thick, hot liquid pumps through his body. Had he not safeguarded against this, not ensured through the constitution that the gate would remain locked at all times? It was not as if he didn't have the support of the rest of the householders. No one wants the place invaded by the riff-raff from the housing estate at the very edge of the neighbourhood. So how on earth did this lot get hold of a key?

It is only when Marie prods him in the ribs, that he realises he has stopped dead in his tracks, transfixed by a smiling Ben who starts towards them holding a bottle aloft.

Do join us for a drink, she calls, it's my house-warming party. I knocked on your door earlier, but you weren't in.

Jeff stares at her uncomprehendingly, and Marie says, But this isn't your house.

There is laughter from the group half-hidden behind the shrubs, and one of the guests gets to her feet with a bowl of olives and a couple of glasses.

Come on people, she says, it's a lovely day at last, the miserable weather's over, so let's drink and be merry.

The voice is foreign, Australian perhaps, or no, South African, and the woman is a large personage with a vast behind and a matching voice. Her face is a funny patchwork — there's no other way of describing it — of dark brown skin with darker stains here and there, and unnatural green eyes.

My cousin's visiting from Cape Town, Ben says, introducing them. Jeff wakes from his trance as she holds a glass of wine before him. He waves it away without thinking.

Look, he hisses, you've been given the regulations, you know this isn't allowed, picnicking, or any such shenanigans in the gardens. I'm afraid you'll have to pack up and carry on in your own house.

We can't possibly do that, Ben replies, my back garden's in a terrible state, full of junk that the previous owners left, and it's too good a day to stay indoors. Why exactly is the green out of bounds? They're public gardens after all, overlooked by all the houses on the square.

Oh no, not public at all; they're private gardens that belong to the house-owners on this square, out of bounds because of a communal decision taken by the Residents' Association. If you want a hand packing things up, we'll gladly help.

That's jolly good of you, but I'm afraid we won't be leaving. You see, I haven't read your regulations, and I wouldn't sign-up to such a decision. My understanding is that each of us owns part of this green so, if you like, my guests could stake out my boundary. Ben turns round to survey the space. Not a bad size, we'll make sure not to step across the line. Beats me why you don't want anyone using the public green, and on a lovely day like this? It'd be great for kids to play in. Not mine of course, and I know yours have fled the nest.

Marie can't be sure, but she thinks she hears an emphasis on the word 'fled', which makes her wince. It's not that ... Marie starts.

But Jeff interrupts. Does the bloody woman not get the difference between public and private? It's obvious, he says. It's private, an exclusive garden; it has to be kept neat. Once residents take liberties, the riff-raff up the road will see it as a free common space to cavort in, and before you know every layabout and drug addict will be sprawling on this grass, littering the place. That's why you have to understand that it's a private green. As for staking out your boundary, it just isn't possible, it's against the spirit of communal gardens.

Well, I'm really sorry to disappoint you, Ben says quietly, but we'll have to stay out here until sunset.

The large cousin turns up the sound of a boombox, rises, and starts dancing in a truly extraordinary manner, arms akimbo and rhythmically twitching each buttock in turn while the rest of her remains perfectly still. Like a grasshopper she sashays towards him, so that

Jeff staggers back, appalled.

Come, he barks at Marie, let's get out of here. But Marie had been pressed into accepting a glass of wine, which she now holds out at arm's length, hoping that someone will relieve her of it. Jeff snatches it from her, brusquely throws the full glass into the currant bush and, taking her by the hand, drags her off. Once indoors, he makes for his chair where he sits in silence while Marie prepares something to eat.

Jolly good, he says mockingly, as he takes a sandwich from the proffered plate. Imagine that, saying jolly good. Bl-bl-bloody Sambos — I'll give them jolly good ...

Now now, Dad, Marie admonishes, you don't mean to say that. Don't upset yourself.

That night, Ben is woken in the small hours by a commotion next door. There is thudding and pounding up and down the stairs, followed by an eerie sound, as if a noisy burglar has unexpectedly lost his nerve and is quietly sobbing a confession. Funny how poorly insulated these houses are against sound. Ben pulls on some clothes, bangs on the neighbours' door and shouts through the letterbox: It's me, Ben from next door. It is some time before Marie answers the door. She stares blankly, helplessly, in a frothy nightdress and bony knees, and waves her hands.

It's Jeff, a heart attack I think, and then he went and fell down the stairs. I don't want him to go, she whimpers.

Jeff is slumped against the wall with a distorted bluish face and a slick of something trailing from his twisted mouth. Ben takes charge. I'm a nurse, she explains. She calls an ambulance, and goes with Marie to the hospital.

I'm useless in crises, Marie says, shaking her head, quite useless; that's what Jeff always says. There is unmistakable pride in her voice. When Ben brings her back, she is quite the invalid, popped into bed with a cup of tea by the brisk nurse.

Marie is embarrassed by the neighbours' attentions.

The brown-black cousin with the big behind brings over first a home-made loaf of rough brown bread and a couple of days later a pot of soup. It's mealie soup she explains, I brought the *samp* from home, and don't you worry, I'm not staying forever; it's only a week before I fly back. Marie would like to refuse the food, it's not as if she can't look after herself, but it is too hard to cross the woman who, standing at her doorstep, fills her in with scary details that she would rather not hear.

Poor old Ben, the woman says, been in exile all these years in Europe, stuck here with that boy who came along just as she thought she was finished with children, and now her Scotsman's gone and died. It's hard not having your family around, although there is the older son, Roddy — he's a published writer, the cousin boasts — but I suppose she can't leave and dump the youngster on him. Ben hasn't always been a nurse. Since her youth she's been a revolutionary, worked for the ANC, when it was the banned national liberation movement, she glosses for Marie who glazes over at all this talk which might as well be in Hottentot language. Marie can't help thinking of the IRA and all that dreadful, bloodthirsty lot.

Oh, she says, you wouldn't have thought Ben to be the killing type.

But the woman claps a presumptuous hand on her shoulder. Now don't you be so foolish, she says, and laughs heartily, Ben wouldn't hurt a fly. As long as its politics are on the left.

The cousin has been tackling the front garden, for which Marie is grateful, even if the woman appears to do it for the wrong reasons. You've got to keep fit and strong and gardening is good exercise, the cousin says in her comic accent. It's a shame, but Marie simply can't remember the woman's name. Something outlandish that begins with a K.

All is not well with Jeff. Instead of recovering as everyone thought he was doing and surely ought to, for that is why they pay their taxes, he has caught an infection in hospital and now is endangered by some condition whose name Marie can't remember. All I know, she says, is that it's filthy, a regular pigsty, and the cousin, who has not been near the hospital, has to agree. If she were to fall ill she'd choose the journey back to Cape Town rather than risk the unhygienic hospitals here.

It is the last straw. Marie has been rendered a gibbering eejit by the complicated turn of events; she is too terrified to drive the short distance to the hospital; she can no longer tell left from right, she's that worried. Ben says there's a bus that stops right at the main entrance, but Marie finds public transport difficult. On a route like that you can just about be sure that some drunk or unwashed person will sit next to you. Ben seems unsympathetic, but Marie must not complain. She's been very neighbourly, a real brick, even if the woman does say 'jolly good'.

When Jeff is finally considered to be out of danger, it would seem that he's gone somewhat muddled. That's what the doctors and nurses say. Marie comes to think of him as being off his trolley. He is confused, and frankly he wears her out with interminable questions. Where is he? What's he doing there? What exactly are the nurses playing at? — over and over again — and once, alarmingly, Who is he? Although that must have been a slip of the tongue. It's not the kind of thing one would talk about to others. She speaks on the telephone to their Ewan and Fiona who live in Huddersfield and London, but lies about Jeff's condition. There is no need, she says, for them to come home; their father will soon be out of hospital and all will be well. It is in Ben whom she finally confides, because she is at the end of her tether: she doesn't know whether she could manage any more visits. It's too much, seeing Jeff as an eejit, he who has always been in charge, who has looked after her. Ben is stern: this is no time to give up, no time for self-pity; she has to keep up the visits, keep talking to him; she, Ben, will go along tomorrow.

Marie has become a child who takes her chastisement as a matter of course.

Jeff greets Ben with exaggerated, stagy politeness. He adjusts his pyjama shirt at the throat — a phantom straightening of the tie — and enquires from his wife who the lovely lady is. Marie is embarrassed. Don't be daft, she says, you know Ben, our new neighbour, and he bows gallantly, thanking her for visiting. Which infuriates his wife. Oh, she says, so we're putting on airs and graces, are we? This appears to throw him into confusion, so that he asks petulantly, Where am I? What is this place?

Och pet, Marie says, it's the hospital, the Royal, you know what it is — not so far from home.

Home, he repeats, and turns to Ben. Thank heavens, he quips, that this isn't home. But then he frowns. Where is the home? Where is the flat?

No, no, Marie explains, we've moved, we're in a house on the square, with the lovely look-out onto the private green with the old oak trees and rhododendrons. Bilsland Square, or Bilsland Street, whatever you want to call it. Home, she says repeatedly, loudly, as if the problem is his hearing.

Ah, he says, so when I get to the door I turn right, do I, into which road? He goes through the directions meticulously, asking and checking, over and over. Ben quips that they won't leave him to find his own way home, upon which he turns to her and smiles admiringly. His eyes linger on her breasts.

Madam, he says, how kind you are, and Marie rolls her eyes and shakes her head.

They have to go through the directions many more times, from turning right at the hospital entrance to turning left into Bilsland Road. There is a brief respite when a nurse brings tea, which he drinks in silence, but when she returns to check something on his chart, he nudges Marie, flicks his eyes at the nurse and cups his hands on his chest, miming the weight of her large breasts. Whoah, he says, have you seen that? So that Marie reddens and admonishes, If you don't behave yourself, you'll never be sent home.

Jeff behaves himself. He straightens up and asks soberly, This home, now can you tell me how I get there? and she explains all over again. Then: Do I want to go home?

Of course you do, she says. It's our lovely home. On Bilsland Square.

And in this place, our home, what do we do there? Jeff asks.

Marie stares at him, bewildered, then affronted. She says curtly, We live there. Dear God — she thinks of *Coronation Street* and hopes he's not going to speak of anything inappropriate.

But what do we do in our home? he persists.

Well, she stutters, well we're retired, so well I ...

It is in his old authoritative voice that Jeff, who is now sitting bolt upright, says, Just tell me woman, speak up, what do we do there, in this home?

Marie looks at him blankly. Tears well up in her eyes, tears of self-pity and incomprehension. Surely she does not deserve this. She would rather he spoke of Saturday-afternoon private activity, after all, than this doolally behaviour. Whatever will the children say seeing their father in a state of such daftness? His eyes are fixed on her; he will not let her go. What do I do there? he demands. She turns imploringly to Ben.

Ben says in a measured voice, It's a house with a lovely garden, Jeff. You and Marie, you both love weeding, or rather gardening. And you sit out on the patio in the lounge chairs the company gave you when you retired. Remember, the blue-and-white striped upholstered chairs, very comfortable they are. That's where you have your G'n'Ts.

Ben may not always have been listening, but Marie's prattling over the fence is certainly coming in handy. Jeff turns to her. His gaze is steady. No, he says emphatically, my question is: what do I do there?

91

Marie has lowered her head; she washes her hands off this humbug, this obscenity. Ben is after all a nurse; she's seen it all, so it's up to her to sort him out, bring him back so to speak.

Ben can tell that Marie, who clutches her arms, has bowed out. How has she got mixed up with these people? How could she be expected to know anything about them? Christ, what does she care? Is it not enough that she speaks of G'n'Ts? They're not her sort of people; they're only neighbours, for God's sake. But just as she decides that she has no choice but to deal with the man, Ben's own head floods with confusing images — of police with dogs, of crouching in the bush with AK-47s and the acrid smell of fear, of Reuben as a baby crying day and night, and Roddy packing his bags, having had enough, whose words pound in her ears: Your world is not mine. I can't live with your past. Yes, there are many worlds, and to return to this one Ben has to scale a high wall, but she slips back, repeatedly, until, after a superhuman effort she reaches the top, back to Bilsland Road where she dredges from her memory a scene from the bedroom window. It is the nurse who says slowly, soothingly, playing for time: Well, you have that nice stone birdbath — you like watching the birds, protecting them from that ginger tomcat who comes prowling ...

It is his eyes that make her stop. For all their weak, washed-out colour they seem to be on fire, popping out of a face flushed in disbelief. His left eyebrow jumps up and down, and the voice that comes out of a mouth curled with disappointment, or distaste, does not belong to Jeff at all.

Gin. Tonic. Weeds. Birds. Cats, he recites. There are equal, theatrical pauses between the next words: Some Bloody Life.

In an agile, youthful movement he slips under the covers, straight as a die, and staring ahead with the quilt pulled up to his chin, says sneeringly, Thank you, ladies. Thank you for your time. Thank you and good afternoon.

Friends And *Goffels*

Julie is married to a pig. That is how it comes to Dot, as a message flashing on a screen, a full sentence that clinches things. There is nothing to be done. She hears the click of a bulging briefcase that brings a long friendship to a close. Or is it an echo of a click? Should she not have known that that's what marriage brings: two people closeted together with no room for a third? Has Julie put the past, which is to say Dot, behind her? And what will she, Dot, do with their history bundled up in a briefcase? Cast aside, she is bereft; her head is in her hands; she doesn't know a thing, except that her heart is broken.

The author of her misery is European, from Scotland, which does not, of course, make him a pig, but he is a pig all the same. And a sadness dense as tonight's starless night wraps itself around Dot who sits at her kitchen table, fighting tears. Light spills from the bedroom so that her shadow on the wall has the hunched, undefined shape of a person parcelled in grief. She might as well make a cup of coffee, no chance of sleeping tonight. Besides, Julie will know that she is now sitting at the kitchen table, drinking coffee, fighting tears, so she will surely want to come over, to talk things through. But Julie is married to a pig. As he stretches, grunts, gets ready for bed, she will not be able to say, or — Dot winces — ask permission to leave. No point in finding a euphemism for a wife's wheedling explanation, the half-truths that must placate a husband — it is no less than asking permission. How could any sensible adult in this day and age buckle down to marriage? Surely this is the point at which Julie would have to choose. Either she would have to announce with car keys in her hand that she'll have to go and see her dear friend, that is Dot, even if it is midnight, and so incur Alistair's anger, or persuade herself that all is well, and thus will not appreciate that she, Dot, is weeping at the kitchen table. Which amounts to no less than casting her aside, dismissing their long history of friendship. By now tears are spilling freely onto the oilcloth. The cloth is her prize possession brought back by Jules last year, a print of lush Rousseauian jungle, the kind of thing you don't find in Cape Town. Never, never, she promises herself, will she marry.

Julie and Dot have known each other since starting at high school. In the hideous blazers of blue, green and red stripes, with hats stuffed in their satchels, they waited for each other at Wynberg station and, stripping ribbons of bark from bluegum trees, dawdled down the wide avenue in order to reach the school gates just as the bell rang. They walked close together, bumping shoulders; they would have liked to hold hands. How often they talked about bunking school together, but they were not the kind of girls who did that, so that the detailed plans were kept open as possibilities, as dreams of freedom.

On the second day at high school, just before registration, there was a charged, preternatural hush until the tall boy, Angus Geddes, scrambled onto the teacher's desk and, egged on by the others, made a formal announcement. Ladies and gentlemen, he said. Amongst them there were a pair of *goffels* who it seemed were to remain in the A class. Imagine, *goffels* in the English-medium Latin class! It was no doubt a mistake, and it was up to the *goffels* themselves to check if they did not in fact belong with the other *goffels* in the Afrikaans-medium woodwork and needlework class, otherwise there might have to be a *goffel* investigation. Each emphatic use of the word brought peals of laughter from the rest. If the girls themselves had not been sure what the word meant, each knew instantly that they were the *goffels*, so they kept

94

their eyes lowered. In the class of posh coloureds Dot and Julie were the only ones who were very dark, had short frizzy hair and flat noses with prominent cheekbones. Everyone knew the indexes of worth amongst coloureds, knew the acceptable combinations of facial features, and that good hair would always override the other disabilities. Dot and Julie did not qualify.

Angus's blazer was long and buttoned up. When he stood up on the table, Dot noted that it reached well below his short summer trousers, so that Angus Geddes seemed not to be wearing any trousers at all. Once he started speaking and used the word for the first time, she dropped her eyes onto the bench where, carved into the wood, was a jagged heart around the initials of JP and SD. Also in blue ink, arranged in zigzag, was a conjugation of 'volo'. Dot felt her elbow twitch, felt the involuntary movement of her right thumb hovering, inching its way to her mouth that snapped open and closed, begging like a fish. She tucked both hands firmly under her buttocks, and rocked from side to side, which would keep the thumb out of reach and help her get through the speech. When Angus Gedddes at last stepped down to triumphant applause, he thrust a revolutionary fist into the air. Dot looked steadily ahead as the heavy brown thighs passed her desk, but she noted that the turn-ups of his short trousers were rolled into an extra turn to make them shorter. When Mr Wilton, the history teacher, arrived with the register, all was restored to the usual quiet murmur.

The girls had already selected their places behind each other in the third and fourth desks of the first row, but had not spoken. After the Geddes speech they kept apart, barely nodding, as if the word *goffel* were contagious and applied only to the other, with whom it would be unwise to associate. They had been declared a pair, but how could that be when they were so very different? They stole surreptitious glances at each other, at the round, moon face and the slit-eyed, bony one. Did *goffelhood* really have the power to override all that difference? In which case, Dot thought, it was not entirely unlike good hair, which made everyone acceptable, attractive. Others in the class, however, felt that they must have known they were a pair, why else had they chosen to sit so close together? Like seeks like, they whispered, and did not notice that Dot and Julie did not speak, that they avoided each other. Later, when a group of girls whispered guiltily about Angus's speech, some wondered if the pair having seated themselves one behind the other had not provoked the *goffel* attack. That, so often, is what these unfortunate ones do: they ask for it, said the tall girl with a horsey face and ponytail. She shook her head so that the luxuriant ponytail swished back and forth.

By the following week when classmates had already gravitated towards each other in pairs or groups, Dot and Julie found themselves during breaks standing against the same far northern fence of the playground. Slowly, imperceptibly they shifted positions until there was nothing left for it — meeting more or less in the middle they had to talk. A bow-legged man with a tray of sweets from the *bubbie's* shop across the road walked up and down the pavement on the other side of the fence. It was hot, and he shouted listlessly: Samoosas, chips, bunnylicks, 'n' creamcakes. Dot remembers that it was she who spoke first. Do you know what are the creamcakes like? she asked. Julie didn't know, and she had already spent her pocket money, so Dot bought one. The man said they could have an extra paper bag, just this once, so they could halve the cake without wasting any crumbs. The cake was layered with leaves of flaky pastry held together with cinnamon syrup, artificial cream, and glacé cherries. Dot said, licking her fingers one by one, It's called a parrot. She had no idea how the word had slipped into her head, but she said emphatically, in what sounded curiously like Angus's voice, That's what we call it. In class, that afternoon, they turned to each other to speak loudly about having had a parrot for lunch; they giggled and shrugged when others asked what that was. The boys at the back, where the Geddes fashion of no-trousers ruled, said that a parrot is the thing to be found in *goffel broekies*, but the pair looked disdainfully down their flat noses and shrugged. But not once, not for many months, did they say the word: *goffel*.

The other girls in the class did not call them names. At first, they steered clear of them in corridors or in the playground, but once Dot and Julie made friends, the others spoke to them on topics such as homework or timetables. Did they speak English at home? Did they belong to the Anglican church? Myra with the swishing hair wanted to know. Dot said yes, which, since they were a pair, went for both of them. In the short intervals between teachers arriving and leaving the classroom, the other girls took out their combs and hair slides, and groomed each other's hair. Like monkeys, Julie whispered. Myra tossed her silky hair vigorously; it flew about like a tail plagued with flies. The ones with smooth wavy hair swopped Alice bands and slides; they discussed the intricacies of rolling and swirling shafts of hair. For Julie and Dot with their short, ironed quills, there was neither combing, nor mirrors propped on the bench. They didn't talk to each other about hair and never mentioned the visible evidence of a hot comb that occasionally, accidentally, singed an earlobe or left a tell-tale scar on the forehead.

It was at the end of the year when there was feverish preparation for the last day of the school year, a day of freedom when everyone dressed up, when the girls spoke of nothing but their new frocks, of how they would have their hair done in flick-ups or French pleats, that Julie asked if Dot had told her mummy what the boys called them. Dot said no, that her mummy wasn't up to it, and then she said it out loud, splitting the word: her mummy did not know what a *gof-fel* was. They fell about laughing. They were *goffels*, and *goffels* wouldn't stoop to the dubious freedom of dressing up on the last day. They came in full uniform, in crisp white shirts, pressed tunics, striped blazers and, for good measure, the crushed hats that no one wore perched foolishly on their heads. The trouserless boys looked on with grudging admiration.

Their student years at UWC, which they called their own *goffel* university, were nothing short of wonderful, in spite of political unrest, or perhaps because of it, because of the need to nail colours to the mast. They sported unkempt Afros and gadded about with the many young men from up country, men like themselves with frizzy hair and cheekbones — except, men were not called *goffels*. With sex so newly invented at the respectable University of the Western Cape, Dot and Julie had no shortage of adventures. For a few years in the eighties, they worked for Umkhonto but were separated from the start, and when it came to the new dispensation, they'd had enough. Neither was interested in political positions. Julie was the cleverer. She left for postgraduate studies in Scotland on a Presbyterian scholarship and stayed. They saw each other from time to time. Dot had visited, and they spoke often on the phone, but no, Julie just didn't see her way clear to returning as yet. But now she was back, with a position at Groote Schuur hospital — and a husband of all things.

Dot met them at the airport. They hugged long and hard and she held Jules away from her to have a good look. I can't believe you've come home, you gorgeous *goffel*, she shrieked, and they collapsed with laughter. But Julie was no *goffel*; Julie looked exactly like Naomi Campbell with long, sleek hair that bounced like a horse's tail, and a complexion that glowed deep honey. They had of course both grown out of *goffelhood* years ago as Black Consciousness swept over the Cape Flats.Then as young women they knew that a little bit of polish made mincemeat of *goffelhood* — Condoleeza Rice even as a toothy teenager would never have been a *goffel* — but Dot could not help being taken aback by the professional makeover. Julie seemed laminated with an overall glossy poly-something substance. Now don't you judge a book by its cover, Julie laughed. It's a change of style; we could all do with a change of style from time to time. And they embraced once more.

Tonight as Dot weeps onto the kitchen table, not uninterested in the lurching about of liquid on the oilcloth, she goes through the logic of the idiom. The point surely of a cover is to give you an indication of what the book is about or what you would like potential readers to think the book is about. Thus one should always judge a book by its cover. But that is disloyal; besides the problem is not Jules, it's the pig husband, who has slyly managed the click of that briefcase from a safe distance — oh nothing to do with him, as he holds up his hands in innocence. Dot's tears rain onto the jungle. With the blade of her right hand she sweeps the liquid across the oilcloth, to and fro. Until she feels the friction, finds that it is quite dry. Not mopped up or absorbed by anything, just gone bone dry.

Dot should have known that all was not well with Alistair Baines. Within minutes of meeting him she understood why the long-forgotten word *goffel* had crept into her speech: Alistair, with his heavy thighs, looked exactly like Angus Geddes morphed into whiteness and adulthood. How could Julie be attracted to someone like that? She had been especially careful not to allow the man's looks to cloud her judgment; that was why she ignored the early signs of piggery. Dot was determined to find him everything she could wish for dearest Jules, and at first, on their sightseeing trips to which she was invariably invited, he had clearly been on his best behaviour. Once or twice Dot called him Angus.

On you go, he laughed good-humouredly, we're all called Angus, we're all the same, some of my best friends etcetera, and Julie, thank God, didn't understand the slip at all. She imagined that someone called Angus had crept into Dot's life, demanded to know all about him, and when she understood it not to be the case, dismissed the slip as a meaningless confusion of names.

Slowly Dot became aware of something building up, something subtle like the change of colour in the sea, the barest darkening of cloud above the mountain before a sudden storm. She had her doubts about the day of the *boerewors*, but decided to make nothing of it. They drove off one morning in search of brunch, before setting off for the house they had rented by the sea. Dot had promised the best *boerewors*, eggs and home-made *roosterbrood*, but first she led them into a street of double-parked cars and impatient drivers through which they had to manoeuvre carefully, and unnecessarily, as it turned out to be the wrong street. Then he simply had to stop, to check whether his car had been scraped. When they finally found the cafe in Observatory to be closed, she rattled the door in disbelief, peered through the window, shaking her head, and only when she got back in the car did she realise that something was wrong. Alistair was a deathly white; the tension was palpable. He beat his fists on the steering wheel.

That's me, that's it, I've had it, he said through clenched teeth. He couldn't do it, couldn't go to the coast, he would go back to the flat and they would just have to drive themselves. Dot was delighted, was about to say that that was fine, that she didn't mind driving, but Julie held up a cautionary hand. It's the migraine, she whispered, but he hissed, That's enough, Jules. Stop right there, Jules, and they drove back in silence.

Julie went inside with him, presumably to help him find medication. Dot had never suffered from a migraine; she supposed the pain to be intolerable; she opened all the car windows to clear the charged air. It took some time for Julie to return, but when she did she was, thank God, smiling. All was well; it had passed, and Alistair was coming along after all. Disappointing, Dot thought, but whatever the 'it' referred to, it seemed to have well and truly passed, for Alistair came shortly after, holding in his hand a scrap of red swimming trunks that were surely meant for a child. Just as well, he said, look what

I've forgotten to bring. And so the skimpy swimming trunks came to serve the function of fig leaf for the genitals, as well as olive branch to smooth over the entire scene. Dot was reminded all the more of Angus. If there was a whiff of sheepishness in his manner, it was soon dispelled by Bob Dylan turned up full blast. Like teenagers they drove with music blaring from open windows. I-d-iot wind, blowing down the smokescreen of my mi-ind, they howled nasally with Bob.

Whilst she saw Julie almost every day, they never got a chance to talk. Alistair even came shopping with them. By no means wealthy, he was generous to a fault, reaching for his wallet well before anyone thought of settling a bar or restaurant bill, and there was simply no way of preventing him from paying. The rand could of course not compete with sterling, but tonight was Dot's treat. She planned the evening: a drink at the fancy new bar jutting out on the cliffs, with a wonderful view of the sunset, then to the Labia to see a film, and finally dessert and coffee at the Waterfront.

The Labia, Alistair spluttered, what kind of name is that. A cinema for dirty old men in raincoats, he laughed.

Funny how one took familiar things for granted, how she had never thought of the name. Tonight she would splash out, and so she ordered champagne, real French champagne. She had never had champagne before, but did it really taste all that different from good old South African Pongracz? she wondered. Of course, Dot didn't know about such things, and really it was the thrill of extravagance that mattered. She thought guiltily, for a fleeting moment, of her parents for whom such indulgence would be unimaginable. They drank on the terrace. She had never seen such tall, elegant glasses hollowed all the way to the base from which the liquor seemed to fountain. Above, a profligate sky was extravagantly streaked with vermilion and gold. The women giggled and bumped shoulders like schoolgirls. Perhaps Alistair was so used to champagne that it meant nothing to him, for they had hardly been there, and well before the bottle was empty, he said that it was time to go, that they would not be in time for the movie. Yes, they would, Julie said, but Alistair said that in order to get good seats they should be early.

Oh there's plenty of time, Dot laughed, waving her arms expansively, have another drink.

Actually there is not — he looked at his watch — and there's parking to take into account. His voice was terse.

Dot held the bottle aloft, twirling it for the pleasure of the fancy label. Half-full? Or half-empty? she joked, but Julie simply held out her glass for a refill. Could they not see the film tomorrow, or some other time? It would be around for a while, Dot said. A strange, quizzical look that she could not read flitted across Julie's face. Julie seemed to be somewhere far away, oblivious to the crisis.

If it was horrible to see the man sink into a childish sulk, there was also satisfaction as Dot watched in amazement his mouth draw downwards, cartoon style, and his shoulders hunch with contained rage. He rose, stormed to the edge of the terrace where he stood for a while with his back to them. The women did not look at each other; they sipped quietly at their drinks, until he returned and broke the awful silence.

What I care about, he said, beating his fist savagely on the artful rusticity of the wall, is steadfastness: sticking to a plan, keeping on time.

But this is Africa, and you're still on holiday, so why not relax, Dot ventured. She thought that Julie's right hand fluttered involuntarily, as if to caution, but no, she wrapped her fingers firmly around the base of the glass.

Perhaps that's what's wrong with your Africa, Alistair snorted. Things might just work out better for your oppressed if they paid attention to time.

He spun out the 'o' as if the rest of the word, oppressed, momentarily eluded him. Which flung the word into another class, less name than a strange category of howling, otherworldly sound.

Julie put her glass on the table and reached for her handbag with an elegant toss of the Campbell mane. Right, let's be off, she said briskly, let's get you to the cinema.

They walked in silence, the man a little ahead of them in what Dot could swear was something of a swaggering gait. Could it be that far from being ashamed, he revelled in the tension?

And then the car would not start. Mocking sounds from the engine and a hiss of rage from Alistair who said repeatedly through gritted teeth, Jesus fucking Christ, Jesus fucking Christ. Until the car gave in, and soon they were bombing along to the Labia. Julie hummed tunelessly. Alistair wanted to know why — Why are you singing Jules? No, she said, it's a Presbyterian hymn that won't let go of me, but I can't remember the words.

After the film, on the way to the Waterfront, they disagreed about *Lost in Translation*. At first about whether Scarlett Johansson is beautiful or not, and then Dot, weary of what seemed like subterfuge, took the plunge: Who cares what the girl looks like, surely what we are trying not to talk about is the disgraceful aspect of this film.

What on earth are you saying? Alistair asked. Dot waited for Julie to say something but Julie would not speak; instead, she took up the humming. Which enraged Dot, drove her to bluntness.

Well, how would you Europeans like to be bothered in this way? How would you like to have your difference from other people made fun of? At the crudest level, take size — do you think the filmmakers weren't banking on the uproarious laughter when whatshisname towers over the little Japanese in the lift? Pathetic. How crass can you get! What's the point of Europeans being hyper-civilised when civility can't stretch to those who are different? No thought there that the little Japanese might find such height grotesque, hey?

Oh lighten up, Alistair said. The trouble with you people is that you're hypersensitive, terrified of being slighted. This society is well on its way to becoming more confident, and then you'll take a more liberal, more urbane view. Relax, one doesn't have to keep an eye on political correctness all the time. Why not talk about the aesthetic qualities, the cinematography, the brilliant ending ...

They drove in silence, which Alistair no doubt read as acceptance of his better judgment, but Dot no longer cared. Julie said nothing, except to give directions, and thank God, they had turned off onto the highway, they had been steered away from further jollity at the Waterfront. No one said a word as Dot scrambled hurriedly out of the car. Alistair drove off with a screech of tyres.

Now dry-eyed, sitting at the table where the puddle of tears has been swallowed by time, Dot would like to withdraw the weeks of friendliness, the smiles, the time she has wasted on Alistair Baines. Julie is married to a pig. And so her heart goes out to Jules who will be lying in the dark in anguished silence. Or, she shudders, may be enduring at this very moment the pig's conjugal rights.

It is this thought that makes her switch off the lights and take herself swiftly to bed in the dark where she gropes for her pyjamas and pulls the covers over her head.

Julie is in her dressing gown at the kitchen table drinking camomile tea. She has always had the ability to spirit herself away to a desert island, to turn the dissonance around her into the swoop of bright parakeets. So she fell asleep instantly, only dimly aware of Alistair by her side, but now, in the early hours, she is wide awake. It just isn't working. Alistair and Dot rub each other the wrong way so they had better be kept apart. Which is a pity, but Dot has always been such a strong, wayward character. She remembers their schooldays, when Julie tried to lean towards her fellow *goffel* — they were a pair for God's sake — Dot kept stubbornly apart, stared resolutely ahead, until she, Julie, broke the silence to ask about the cake. The parakeet, she tried to christen it, as they fell about laughing, but Dot said no, that was too long a name, that it was a parrot.

Perhaps it is foolish to imagine that a friendship can be sustained over years of separation; one can't, after all, expect things to stay the same. There are things Julie supposes that she no longer understands; she has been away too long; she does not, for instance, understand why sensible, otherwise responsible people drink unhealthy amounts of alcohol and then drive their cars. It doesn't make sense. Julie does not like to dwell on matters that puzzle her, not here at home where she belongs. Would people not say that she has lost her roots?

Roots — she wonders if that is not at the root of it all. Perhaps Dot is peeved that she has said nothing about the book of poetry she had given her on the very day they arrived. Julie has never liked poetry, never understood the short, coded lines, and now a whole fat book to wade through. She can't remember the name of the poet, but the book seems to be about traditional Khoisan stuff— moon, stars, weird mumbo-jumbo. She would not necessarily find such things uninteresting, but poetry, for heavensakes, what on earth could she say?

That evening, standing on the terrace with a blood-red sun hovering on the sea, Dot told a story about a neighbour. Julie thought she looked lovely in that pink light, thought how she deserved a good man, wondered why she had missed the boat. Always a good storyteller Dot was, but she must have forgotten that Julie had been there, or perhaps she believed that Julie had not overheard the conversation on the doorstep. Trivial perhaps, but Dot chose to tell Alistair about the neighbourhood-watch that people in her street were trying to set up, about the woman who knocked on her door and asked to speak to the owner of the house. Alistair did not understand so that she explained tetchily: Don't you see, a *goffel* opened the door in the middle-class neighbourhood, and the blond dame didn't ask whether the *goffel* was the owner of the house, she just assumed that I wasn't. Must have thought I was the char. She spoke very much like you — Scottish, I suppose.

Yes, I see, Alistair said, yes there've always been many Scots in these parts. Dot looked at him scathingly; it seemed that he had failed a test.

Julie had explained to Alistair that she would pick Dot up early, that they would have coffee together. On their own, she had to say emphatically, because Alistair, bless him, did not always get things right. Oh, he meant well, and insisting on always coming along was of course about accepting Dot as *their* friend, but Julie did so want to see her old friend on her own.

How could Dot have forgotten that she, Julie, had been there when the woman knocked? From the kitchen where they had been drinking coffee she heard clearly the woman introduce herself as Fiona from number thirty-two, and explain the neighbourhood-watch scheme; she hoped that Dot would put the sign in her window. There was surely no question about who the owner of the house was; it all sounded quite amiable. It is true that Dot was brisk in her replies, explained that she had a friend round, but the story she told Alistair — it wasn't right.

Julie's head feels heavy, she really needs her sleep, and this is not the time to rake things over. It will all have blown over by the morning. And perhaps the woman, the neighbour in the story — perhaps that was another one. She yawns. She and Dot have been together since way back; there is no question of them not being friends forever.

The double beep of the cell phone drills through a dream about a stampede of trouserless men with fat brown thighs. Or at least that is how Dot recollects a dream that eludes, that promises to piece together, only to fall apart once more.

Dot sits up and checks the time. It's three o'clock. She

takes a gulp of water before reading Julie's SMS — is that all?

Let's all try to be more tolerant. Not used to this drinking and driving.

A text message — is that all?

She leaps out of bed. So that is what it amounts to, being married to a pig, consorting with an Angus, and turning yourself into Naomi Campbell — the glorious *goffel* days have gone for good. She throws on her clothes. At the kitchen table covered with lush jungle print, where Dot sits dry-eyed, she struggles with the notion of pallid tolerance. Drinking and driving, yes of course, but tolerance — and she beats her fist on the table — she'll have no truck with wishy-washy tolerance.

The noise startles the ghost of a bird, a bright parakeet, who darts from Rousseau's jungle, settles for a second as a clearly drawn shadow on the wall, then vanishes.

Trompe L'Oeil

One knows what to expect from a man who wears a blazer, for the blazer is designed to announce the wearer's unassailable authority. The brass buttons and double-breastedness confer both authority and probity upon the wearer, and what is more, they keep a man on his toes. The double-breasted blazer does not brook investigation. Just as it does not permit slouching, a leaning this way or that; rather, it bellows a no-nonsense clarity of purpose guaranteed by the combination of sober navy-blue with sportive brass buttons that declares its difference from the staid traditions of the suit. Thus does the blazer blaze the wearer's ready-made integrity. In its signifying function, it is not unlike denim, which once spoke so unashamedly of permissiveness and subversion, of a brazen disregard of order, that it had to be rescued and recuperated by the fashion industry. There is of course no danger of the blazer being appropriated in that way.

The two men in representative blues are discussing secularism. They stand at the railings of the grand house, admiring the sublime view, the tie-dye blue of the sea into which a bloody sun is about to plummet. X, in denim, shifts his weight, bracing himself for a lecture from the blazered man by his side. He ought to have found an excuse to leave when Y arrived but, never having met anyone like Y, he is at the same time fascinated by the man.

Gavin deplores this kind of thing, fiction that claims to say something significant about the real world. These people should stick to stories, events and characters, rather than rummage through stale stereotypes and imagine that something new has been forged. He has no objection to a good old-fashioned yarn, that is, when one can find the time for reading fiction, but this pompous stuff... Why on earth does Bev think that he would be diverted by it? She ought to know that he sees through this kind of thing — platitudes passed off as profundities.

It is the beginning of a short story by Roddy What's-his-name, the Scottish writer they met at the Study Centre in Italy — at least, RP are his initials, and the story appears to be set at just such a place. That, presumably, is why Bev, who knows that Gavin has neither time for nor truck with fiction, thinks he would want to read it. Bev, who unfortunately had nothing much to do at the Centre, was rather taken in by the chap with his funny, sing-song Glasgow accent and the olde-worlde 'ayes' and 'buts' which, if you asked Gavin, was pure affectation. Surely educated Scots don't speak like that.

You're a colonial at heart, Gavin teased Bev. He could not quite bring himself to say so, but her interest was surely in the young man's parentage — a Scot with a South African mother — as if they did not have enough of all that tiresome stuff at home.

So, should we be reading you? What is it you write about? Gavin had asked Roddy loudly across the expanse of dinner table. The young man seemed taken aback, embarrassed, as if it were a faux pas on Gavin's part, which was of course a piece of nonsense. He was only asking him to speak of something that already existed in the public domain; besides, that's why they were there, to get on with their work and, surely, to speak about it.

Och, this and that, you know, Roddy stuttered. Nothing much, nothing other than you'd expect but.

They sparred regularly over dinner. The young chap, like most young people nowadays, had astonishing gaps in his knowledge that Gavin felt compelled to address.

Don't mind the professor, Bev laughed.

The white man's burden, Roddy quipped. Where would I be without the help?

Gavin was irritated. Why behave as if South Africa had not lost its pariah status? He said out loud, Why not take your cue from Mandela? Heard of *ubuntu*? Gavin had just that day read in *The Times* an English political commentator ridiculing the word, citing its transliteration as so much meaninglessness, so that he, Gavin, for once would refuse to instruct, refuse to be the source of information, as the young man looked blankly at him. This time the boy — who with tilted head seemed to be waiting for an explanation — could look it up himself. But Bev, who often got the wrong end of the stick, frowned and said that it would not be necessary. She seemed to be taken in by the young man's shallowness. There was something about him that Gavin couldn't fathom, couldn't put his finger on, except that he was irritating in a quiet, needling sort of way. Roddy had provoked him into saying that the imagination is overrated, that writers' 'work' cannot compare with the thinking required for historical or philosophical research. Which he supposes is an extreme position that he does not actually, or fully subscribe to, although God knows it does contain an element of truth. And they only have themselves to blame. Even at the University here in Cape Town the writing of fiction and poetry is now called 'research'. It should keep the travel costs and library budget down, plumbing the depths of their own psyches, he recently joked with a sceptical colleague in the English department.

Still, in spite of the arty fellows, the Study Centre had been a wonderful gift. It was good to meet other scholars, and without the concentrated period of writing, the uninterrupted days and the world warded off by a phalanx of efficient staff, he would not have arrived at such astonishing insights, and finished the work in the short sabbatical. And now the monograph on nineteenth-century European settlement in the Eastern Cape has, just as he expected, won a well-deserved prize. For the truth of the matter is that there's so much shoddy scholarship about — the universities in this country are simply no longer the places of learning that they once were.

111

Gavin loves Saturday evenings like this. Bev cooked a superb dinner of *kingklip* for just the two of them, and after his customary clearing of the dishes, he settled in his chair in this comfortable sitting room where, looking out onto the garden, they read or listen to music. The rain in winter may be relentless, but in summer there is nothing to beat this house. Last year he had the entire wall replaced with sliding glass doors so that the frangipani and nicotiana waft into the room, and the brook around which the garden is structured babbles cheerfully. Now, as they listen to Beethoven in the twilight, inside and outside slide into each other. He lights a citronella candle, just in case. There is nothing like watching from the comfort of upholstered chairs a pale moon mature in the sky. Just the two of them.

Gavin wishes that Bev had not left the magazine section of the newspaper on his chair. The *Mail & Guardian* had printed the short-listed story from *The Guardian* competition. He supposes they are short of news. He has flicked through the story, gratified to find his views on contemporary writing confirmed: passable, if predictable descriptions of the setting at the Italian Study Centre — the roar of the sea competing with that of the traffic, the rustle of pine trees, the grand house and elegant lunches at the large perspex table on the terrace, the mildly diverting exchanges between characters. And, predictably, the Ligurian *trompe l'oeil*. Are writers not supposed to use their imaginations, invent, for God's sake? What is the point of simply transferring from the everyday, from what happens to be within view, or hearing, to the page? Gavin shakes his head. It is the same problem he has with photography, and as far as he can gather no one has yet satisfactorily explained how such documentation succeeds in illuminating the human condition. The discussion in the story of colonial genocide is marginally more interesting. Roddy's character, much given to shaking his head vigorously, says:

No, no, no, such speculations are painful to those of us who know something about history. Let me take you through the arguments.

Gavin must hand it to him — the positions are surprisingly well-presented, logically argued. But where is the art in that? He chuckles at the dialogue, not least because, for all the sardonic tone, young RP has clearly learnt some lessons in history from their dinner-table discussions. But all through the Beethoven sonata, something has been niggling, and now Gavin finds himself picking up the paper once again.

Bev, who is doing the crossword, looks up to see Gavin shaking his head. Oh dear, she should not have given him the Arts Supplement with RP's story; she is not in the mood for a diatribe on art and knowledge. It had been such a joy having Roddy at the Centre. Nearly two years ago — and Bev still savours his frank interest in her, his careful consideration of what she so haltingly had to say. You should write, he said, which made her blush. And so she tried, sat down with pen and notebook, and forced herself to write, but that precisely was the problem — it was a matter of forcing out the words so lacking in flow that such a business could not be called writing. She ought to have found the courage to talk to the young man about it, but the time never seemed right. Then, after realising that she had struggled for two consecutive nights to find outfits with which to wear again the necklace that he had complimented her on, she felt ashamed, and for a few days avoided him. I'm old enough to be his mother, she said aloud to herself, and felt even sillier. Of course she needed no such admonishment. Was it because of the mother, the woman from the tip of Africa, more or less Bev's age, that he took such a kindly interest in her?

Pass the mulk, he mocked at breakfast. You sound just like my mum.

How often she wished that she could ask about the woman, the revolutionary mother, but it would have been

113

too difficult. All she could hope for is that he had not read it as indifference, that he had understood how she was trapped by all that complicated history.

Does Bev really expect Gavin to read the story? She knows what he thinks of contemporary writing, of the hype, as he calls it, the media-driven culture industry. Perhaps she wants him at least to believe that the boy is well regarded, that she had not been stupid in admiring him. Now, looking up again, she notes his frown, the livid colour, and feels a shiver of terror.

Gavin is a celebrated historian who, before the end of his first year as a student, had already earned the label of 'bright'. From the start he was considered a star, a catch, and Bev was certainly envied for having been chosen by someone with the unusual combination of being bright, handsome, and a rugby star. Envied when they married. She lists the things that others must have foreseen: for bearing the name that appears on the cover of the well-reviewed books, for foreign travel that comes with a prestigious Chair in History, for the issue of marriage, their lovely boys, both away at university — all these things must have been there as embryos, little bloody specks, contained in the albumen of brightness. She tosses the word about and summons its synonyms: vivid, luminous, brilliant, blazing. Blazing, as in blazer.

It was the summer of 2000, when arguments were trawled out once more on whether the new millennium does not actually start in 2001, and the magazines offered yet again advice on new resolutions, starting afresh, on new directions and new wardrobes, and on how they had escaped computer meltdowns by the skin of their teeth, so that, when Gavin received his letter of acceptance from the Italian Foundation and invited her along, she looked upon it as a beginning. At least for herself.

Oh, you should come, he said, it could be something of a holiday for you — no cleaning or cooking — and besides, what on earth will you do with yourself, kicking your heels here for two months on your own?

114

It is true that she is often lonely. After all the chores, the reading of a novel, a newspaper, and the planning of dinner, the afternoons stretch endlessly, forlornly ahead of her. Then she wanders through the house from room to room, sits for a while surveying what is hers, theirs. So much stuff — chairs, cupboards, framed prints, beds, rugs, crockery, so many different patterns to memorise and recall, and Bev would wonder: What to do? What to do with it all, what to do with herself? When the children were still there, at school, she had on occasion asked other mums what they do when all the chores are done, but it turned out that chores are never done. Afternoons of pacing the floor, waiting for the hours to pass, could, it turned out, be avoided, but she lacked the necessary imagination, was no good at thinking up new forms of housekeeping, and Gavin certainly did not think her amiss in the running of the house. They have never had servants, and after the children left, they dismissed the char who came once a week for three hours. They would not be typical South Africans, Gavin said, though Bev worried about the hungry women who knocked on her door for bread, and who offered, in exchange, to wash the windows she had just buffed into gleaming mirrors. She could not say with pride, I've cleaned them myself; instead, she said that she already had a cleaner. Bev found that peeling potatoes in the early afternoon for dinner that night, or kneading bread for tomorrow, or pickling lemons for the summer, simply shifted the dark hole of time further on into the days, the weeks, the months ahead. The hours remained so many beads stuck on a rusty abacus, unwilling to slide along. There was no escaping the time in which she floundered, in which her spirit grew thin, spread through the house, spread effortlessly over all the dust-free surfaces of cupboards and chairs and beds, seemed to evaporate, leaving her light-headed so that she would have to sit down and sternly summon back the Bev who sorted out the laundry into white and dark, cooked balanced meals, and settled electricity bills.

Gavin's suggestion had made sense. She would view the fellowship in Italy as an experiment with unpunctuated time, unmarked by chores, which would settle things for good. She would read novels about other mild-mannered women; perhaps try poetry; read up on the history of the area, the architecture and the dazzling *trompe l'oeil* of Liguria, in which, maybe, a lesson lurked. Bev, who managed to get lost in Cape Town in spite of Table Mountain, toyed with the idea of day trips to other towns. Would she have the courage to take such risks? She took lessons in Italian, which for some months guaranteed the shift of an abacus bead from 3 to 4p.m. Gavin smiled distractedly at her preparations.

Did he really want her to come to Italy? Would she not be in his way, cramp his style?

He deplored the vulgar expression. Of course he wanted her to come. She had never been in his way and he knew he could rely on her to be sensitive to his needs. Of course — he had no misgivings at all. Few women your age look as good as you do, he said, having thought about the expression and decided there was an entailment that warranted the reply. But what was his style? He supposed himself to be a solid, old-fashioned sort of man, a family man, who dressed soberly in a navy-blue blazer, and perked up remembering that actually, his hair was rather fine, no loss there, so that he did not have to worry about styling strands across a thinning patch as so many men of his age do.

Gavin, struggling with the story, is not surprised that his thoughts have wandered. Nevertheless, he will read on. Bev will be disappointed if he doesn't finish it. Fortunately it is the sort of thing that one could easily skim, skip a phrase, a sentence or two.

For all Y's authority, the child, the palimpsest of a boy who is afraid of pigeons, persists; it rises like a blush below the elegant silver hair, so that the fleeting look translates into a message of panic, a plea to his wife. Who will act, will leap to his side to steer him away from menace, from the portly

pigeons that strut self-importantly, or the cool, compre-
hending look of the gauche young man who will not take his
word, who tries to interrupt.

I'll check it in Brewer's, the young man stutters, when
Y has already explained the mythological origins, has
given a fuller explanation than any contained in a dic-
tionary.

Bev yawns. Through heavy eyelids she watches Gavin
wriggle in his seat and reach for his drink before he turns
back a page to re-read.

At the Study Centre, Bev did not find it easy to be a
spouse. She ought to have been used to the condition, but
there she was something like an uninvited guest, a free-
loader, a charity case, or so she thought the serving staff
viewed her. They grimaced at her poor Italian and made
no effort to speak slowly, but Gavin said that she was
imagining things, that her sensitivity was a symptom of
the colonial cringe.

And how did Madame spend the day? the Czech historian asked.

She giggled, Oh this and that, explored the gardens;
she did not believe that he really wanted to know.
Already his eyes darted about in search of escape. She
was grateful for the writers and artists who brightened
the evening dinners. They did not seem so serious, and
Bev thought, Why not? Why not try her hand at writing,
nothing serious, of course, just a bit of fooling around
with words, see if she could sketch a scene. But the words
she knew were dense forests through which a path had to
be beaten and Bev lacked the strength. One evening
before dinner, after a tiring day with pen and blank
paper, she sought out Roddy; she would talk to him about
writing. He had just joined a group standing around awkwardly with their drinks. He said that such an affair
where you were expected to circulate was called a
stonneroonie in Glasgow. The drink in hand would loosen
their limbs and tongues and steer the prattling party-
goers about the room, and he demonstrated with a silly

walk and a flash of teeth that got everyone laughing, so that Gavin too rose to join them.

Gavin said that he had read that day that so many million works of fiction were published per year. Did they not think it terrible, all this production of novels, with which to fill the world?

Roddy smiled. Publishers would not publish books that they did not think they could sell, he said.

Well, I call it shameful, wasteful, Gavin persisted, the sheer amount of pulp produced, tossed into a benighted world — I am of course not speaking of great literature — and then others have to read it all.

In the larger scheme of things where men join armies and go out to shoot people they don't know, the harmless, solitary pleasures of reading and writing could hardly be called shameful. In fact, they should be encouraged. And not many of us are able to read or write great literature. We have to make do...

No, no, no, Gavin interrupted, but Roddy, the conscientious fellow, turned away with drink in hand to circulate according to the rules of the stonneroonie.

It turned out that the spouse's unstructured time at the Study Centre was only such within the fixed parameters of set mealtimes and Gavin's working routine. Saturday and Sunday afternoons were reserved for sightseeing. Bev spent her free hours lying on the dirty beach where the seaweed had started rotting, staring aloft at the growing white line drawn by departing aircrafts, the bright point of a pen driven inexorably across the blue slate sky. Purposeful. Leaving behind a clear message. That was what it ought to be like, she thought. The notebook by her side was a mess of half-finished sentences, vigorous scrubbing out, and so very little left of her efforts. She would have to tear out the pages, destroy them; she kept her labour with words on the beach a secret. If only she could knock up something like the *trompe l'oeil* window on the narrow building that she passed on the way to the shore. The building, wedged snugly into the fork of two streets, boasted a window whose lime green curtains were captured flapping gaily, and permanently, in an imagined breeze. Momentary deception of the eye — that was all she aspired to. It was not as if Bev imagined herself a Virginia Woolf or a Nadine Gordimer; she had nothing of importance to say; she didn't expect any more of her own attempts than to brighten up a street corner or to help one forget the stifling heat for a brief, illusory moment. And still writing eluded her.

Three meals per day spent with other fellows was trying. Gavin preferred Bev to sit by his side at lunchtime, so that he could report on the morning's work, and that was preferable to making small talk with the professors. But were they not expected to circulate? Who cares, he said loudly, about couples having to separate at table. He didn't, he added in the silence that followed. He had chosen her, Bev, to share his life with, so stuff the rules. And over lunch he discussed a trip they would have to make to the Eastern Cape, a matter of research that had cropped up. Damn, he would have to leave that chapter for lack of evidence, but he had no doubt that he would find it, that things would work out as planned. Bev hoped that there would be a chance to talk with Roddy about the *trompe l'oeil* of the region, but sitting as he did across the divide of the large table she did not have the courage to raise her voice.

How extraordinary, Roddy said after dinner one evening, that you two should do everything together, that after all these years you still seem to like each other. A good advertisement for marriage if ever I saw one. You must know everything there is to know of each other.

He was single; nothing so far had worked out for him. No one to cramp his style, Bev thought. Gavin took the young man's expression of surprise for admiration or envy.

Thirty years at the end of this month, he proffered, so it isn't surprising that we are so close, that we do everything together.

119

We had a wonderful time in Genoa today — the Palazzos Rosso and Bianco, San Lorenzo cathedral... Bev feared that he would list all their sightseeing, so that she interrupted, murmured that yes, they've been so lucky, together for thirty years. But Gavin shook his head emphatically.

No, no, no, not lucky. It takes some thought, some backbone to keep a marriage working in these pressured times.

Y shakes his head. No, no, no, he says.

He has two ways of starting. If not the multiple 'No's, his opening would be: Of course, of course, which involves an equally vigorous shaking of the head, and really there is no way of knowing how the man chooses between the two since both are followed by an invitation to infer that his knowledge and understanding are boundless, that the other person's naivety is a given.

X frowns thoughtfully while the lecture on cultural difference is being delivered. The new Pére Ubu, he thinks, blazered, and buffed by the academy. 'Bunkum' — delivered in his mother's no-nonsense guerrilla style as she looks her interlocutor straight in the eye — that's what he ought to say. Instead, he smiles. Perhaps it's all about personal vanity: Y shakes his head to draw attention to his handsome, full head of once-blond hair now elegantly silvered with age. Common vanity, a vigorous nod at Mother Nature who has always been kind to him, whom he has come to rely on.

Gavin would like to stop reading this odious story, but something over which he has no control drives him on. It is the same morbid fascination with which he examines in the mirror his mosquito bites, the swollen sacs of poison that drag his face into skew-whiff distortions, the same absorption in something that he knows to be temporary. Like mosquito bites, this story will eventually disappear without trace. There is no need to be upset by these facile words, by the ravings of a limited mind. But something niggles, a sense of something unspeakable woven into these sentences that Gavin can't bring himself to draw out into the light. And a monstrous sense of shame creeps up lividly from the open neck of his shirt to his very brow where it settles in the luxuriant hair. He steals a look at Bev. Does Bev know of the thing hidden in this story? Bev sits with her hands in her lap, her eyes glazed, her head tilted. Most likely she has not yet read it, or not read it carefully, in which case he must protect her from it. He must find a way of hiding and destroying the paper. Gavin wonders if RP has interrogated his own use of initials — X, Y, Z indeed, instead of naming his characters. Pathetic. No doubt such cowardice passes for postmodern ingenuity. Speed reading is all this story deserves. His eyes skim across a couple of paragraphs until he is held spellbound.

> *The suites are partitioned at the bathroom wall, which ensures privacy, protects them from each other's sounds. Except in the bathroom itself where the partitioning wall is less solid than one would expect. There, occasionally, above the sound of rushing water he witnesses the lie that is Y's perfect marriage. He lies rigid in his bath and tries not to splash, the better to hear that voice of reason bark at Z, laugh cruelly at her quiet, timid explanations. She would be cringing at the menace that rises above the angry rush of water. X hears the wife's whimpers of fear or her clipped anger, and finds himself inventing a dialogue around which to weave a story. More than once the stifling of dry sobs like hiccups. The bathroom is also a place in which to retreat, he supposes, but then the entry of another, the unmistakable No, no, no and the slamming of doors. So much for that smiling marriage.*

Gavin sits bolt upright in his chair as the monstrous thing claws its way out of the print, and hisses. How low can a writer stoop? He is not surprised to find that the chap eavesdropped on their conversations in the bathroom, but how dare he misrepresent their marriage in this way? How dare he be so cruel to Bev, poor gullible Bev who wouldn't harm a fly, who had shown the chap every kindness, and who had listened attentively to his pretentious prattle? The thing slithers under Bev's chair where it hides. The young man simply has no sense of morality, of decency. If Gavin has never balled a fist in his life, he is close to it; if he were to walk into Roddy What's-his-name now, there'd be no accounting for his actions. There is a bitter taste in his mouth. Fiction, my foot, he snorts with disgust.

Why did Bev give the offensive story to Gavin?

She had read it whilst making the dinner. That after-noon she started early, intending also to get the bean soup ready for the following day, and whilst she stirred the onions, making sure that they caramelise rather than burn, she read the paper held aloft in her left hand. When the beans had been added and the stock heaved energetically in the pot, Gavin came into the kitchen, so that she folded the paper in half, put it on the wooden counter and swiftly transferred the bubbling pot of soup onto the wad where she continued stirring. There was some spillage but never mind, it didn't matter, she would bin the paper anyway. And now watching Gavin grow red with rage, she can't tell why she hadn't binned it after all.

Bev expected the story to be about something real, in fact, to be somehow connected with Roddy's mother. Would that not have been why it was printed in the *Mail & Guardian*? Once, he asked her about the Eastern Cape, where he said his mother had known Steve Biko and spent some months in gaol. He hoped to visit the region early next year, a research trip, although he hoped also to meet family — he owed it to his mother, he muttered. So, was the mother dead? Bev wondered. She nodded; she felt for him. Why then was she unable to ask about the mother? Instead, she waved at the Czech historian hov-ering under the great palm tree, who rightly read it as an invitation to join them. Her voice was thick with shame as she said, Poor Pavel, how lonely he seems to be.

Even a cursory look at the story must have given Bev an idea of the thing, Gavin decides. He understands her hurt, her need for him to explain the ugliness away. That is surely why she has left the paper on his chair.

You know why he hates us? Prejudice. We are white South Africans of a certain age, the ready-made pariah. Gavin's voice is unnaturally calm.

But he doesn't hate us, Bev says, oh no, not at all. We spoke quite a bit in the end, quite frankly of the bad old days, you know.

Which goes to show how innocent Bev is, how simple and good-hearted, so that a rush of affection mingles with the bile in his throat. He would like to place both hands around the chap's scrawny neck and slowly squeeze the life out of him. Not that he cares about the pathetic characterisations, the heinous misrepresentation. No doubt the story has been short-listed as an act of positive discrimination — they have strict quotas in Britain these days and of course South Africa, ever the colonial mimic, is following suit in that direction. The meanness of it all, the folly, beggars belief. Gavin's bile subsides. Why should he care about such badly-written nonsense, a story so patently devoid of imagination? He will skip to the last paragraph just see how the artless thing gets wrapped up, check on the direction of the man's malice. Actually, Gavin often sneaked a look at the last page of a novel, even if across the unread pages the words did not mean much.

He is transfixed by her. The lovely red hair tumbles in luxuriant waves in the lamplight that pools above her head. Her eyes are half-closed as she listens to the Moonlight Sonata and her hands, still youthful, lie serenely in her lap. Her face is composed, which gives her the beauty that she does not quite manage in daylight. As the music moves into a crescendo he watches, spellbound, her left hand rise slowly as if in a trance, watches it move mechanically to the coffee table by her side where it falls precisely upon the glass paper-weight, cupping it in the dome of her palm. It has a green eye in the centre, and from the pupil rays of colour shoot into the glass. He watches her lift her hand, in balletic slow motion, the weight of the glass palpable in her dreamlike movement. Her arm is raised, stretched well above her head when she leans back and, like the skilled netball player of her schooldays, aims for the centre of the French window, drawn across into a double pane. It shatters into a million pieces as the glass eye crashes into reinforced glass, the mosaic spreading and crackling eerily, and beyond it a full trompe l'oeil moon disperses into a million fragments before it skids away across the sky. Her arm is still raised and the glass jewels are still dropping like hailstones out of a clear sky when he rises, crosses the jewel-studded threshold to find some air for his choked lungs from which an eerie sound escapes.

Outside the sky is spangled with stars. There is also the pointed red light of an aeroplane finding its way expertly across the chaos of lights and stars, straight as a die as it dips towards its destination.

Nothing Like The Wind

The sound of traffic is nothing like the wind.

Elsie knows that. She's not mad, deranged, out of her head, *bedonderd*; all the piglets are safely in the pen, but what she hears all the same is the wind, rushing between outbuildings, sweeping through mimosa trees, through that place. The scene, fully converted from sound, is clear and detailed: Rover's chipped enamel plate lies on its side by the shed door; the wheelbarrow waits with Jafta's blue overalls slung over the handle; shrivelled mimosa balls are blown into an arced ridge against the wall of the stoep. Elsie likes Miss Smith's story of a butterfly's wing at the tip of Africa that triggers a hurricane on a still European shore, infinitesimal, but indisputably there as a reason. The conversion of traffic on the Great Western Road is equally precise, something like a mathematical calculation, or a grammatical exercise, like turning a sentence into the passive voice, into indirect speech, or another tense. But she does not want to know why the sound of traffic translates itself into the moan of the wind through that distant landscape. Only sometimes, no doubt to throw her off the track, another world engulfs her, a vague distant one where things remain out of focus, and then it is the sound of waves that roars in her ears, high as houses, that is, like these tall sandstone Glasgow tenements — houses stacked on top of each other. Could there be an ark drifting beyond reach in the distance, light as a paper boat? The sound of waves allows her to fill in the scene with anything at all. Nothing like the wind, where the place is fixed, the Karoo scene of stones and quiver trees, the outbuildings and, of course, the farmhouse itself.

Who is she? She is Elsie, the fifth-former, who goes out every day to classes in sociology and poetry and some other things she doesn't care two hoots about. It is much better now than last year when she arrived to that din of strange speech, the embarrassment of teachers trying to make themselves heard above the noise, the paper darts in damp corridors, and above all, being turned out during intervals into the cold where the sandwich would drop out of your numb hands and the clutch of Pakistani girls huddled against the same wall would try not to stare. In a couple of years she'll go to Glasgow Uni like the others and no doubt some of them, or perhaps just a nice quiet girl like herself, her father says, will become a friend. But first there is surely the problem of class. Her father says nonsense, our family's always been a good class of people, of good Scottish blood, but he knows nothing about the topography of class, the complexities of double-barrelled terms: lower-, middle-, or upper-middle class, and then the possibility of upper- or lower-working class. He does not know that it is different over here, that difference, no longer simply identified by surface, the colour of skin or texture of hair, is hidden. Elsie suspects that they are either upper-working class or lower-middle class, but the difference between the two, in spite of all her sociology, would seem to be discernable to natives alone who talk about these things in code. Anyway, whatever it is, she would by dint of Uni be propelled into middle-middle. Which she understands to be a solid, comfortable place from which you can't escape. Where she imagines herself sitting with legs astride, like a boy, like Freddie, her hands restless on her knees.There will be the satisfaction of not occupying the same world as her father, except, when the wind roars in her ears and she is transported to that place, she cannot be sure that they are not both forever fixed in the same sphere, miles away at the tip of Africa.

Elsie, sitting with her knees squeezed tightly together, listens to the traffic on the Great Western Road. She tracks the sound of a double-decker bus along the incline from Kelvinbridge, an incline that pedestrians may barely be aware of, but as the traffic lumbers up towards the robots — she must remember to say traffic lights — the sound betrays the gradient. Just about by the post office, she guesses, there is the business of changing gear, of vehicles revved up and whining towards Byres Road, so that the wind whooshes with a whistle across the *veld*, across the yard, through the outbuildings and the workers' shacks, the rickety deal-wood of doors with cracks and gaps through which it weeps like an orphan. Doors quite unlike these massive, triple-locked monoliths that fit tightly into their frames. Everything in this small country is heavy: doors that cannot be elbowed open; huge tall stone buildings that cast shadows over each other.

It doesn't mean that things back home are rickety, Freddie said defensively, it's just that the cold has to be kept out over here, and doors and windows have to fit snugly to prevent draughts. Which is a problem, as even the bathroom window can't be opened without difficulty. Elsie has become adept at controlling her bowels and bladder; she shudders at the thought of her father's excreta, and after he's been will wait hours for miserly fresh air to seep into the lavatory. But the cold air cannot be kept out, so that here people are always shouting to each other: Shut the door. Her father says that people sit by themselves behind shut doors, which makes them forget about having neighbours and encourages low-down, secretive behaviour. It certainly encouraged Freddie.

The old boy — that is how Elsie thinks of her father — has nevertheless taken to fighting draughts. He goes to the market on Saturdays at the Barras in search of draught excluders, which he says can be covered in fancy fabric to match their furnishings. Things are not easy over here; they are no longer well-off and must do without servants. He hasn't found anything for the draughts; instead, every week he returns with yet another object in brass. A collection, he says, that's what it's going to be. On Sundays, he takes to them vigorously with Brasso and a yellow rag, and polishes away at his bargains until they shine: useless containers with decorative squiggles in which the polish hides until the incisions are reversed into grayish lines of build-up. Elsie would like to dig out the gunge from the little brass bell that rests snugly in its cup, but these things belong to him. For summoning the servants, her father laughs. When they first arrived, a sullen charlady came on Thursdays, but she wore neither apron nor overalls. She muttered to herself above the sound of the vacuum cleaner and whooshed through the flat in less than an hour. When he put out the brass, only a few items then, she looked puzzled for a moment, then simply said, No chance wee man. It turned out, though, that they couldn't afford even such a person, besides, her father said, white people are clearly not cut out for domestic work and as far as he could see there were no available black women hanging about the streets. Freddie took to pulling faces behind his back, twisting an index finger at his temple to indicate madness whenever the old boy said anything at all, and much as she despised her brother she had to agree that their father invariably spoke nonsense. Nowadays he rarely speaks and for that she is grateful.

Elsie checks the front door once more. She can't remember whether she has locked it. She has become forgetful, feels the passage of time minute by minute, feels herself growing old, especially in the new gold-rimmed glasses dispensed by the National Health. Indoors she has taken to draping an old shawl over her shoulders as she snuggles up to the radiator, listening to the wind. A sage-green shawl like Granny Reid's, her real granny with apple cheeks, smelling of vanilla, and shuffling across the kitchen to produce with shaky hands from a wooden barrel boer-biscuits large as saucers. Elsie checks that the door is safely barred against the wind, Granny's kitchen door.

The old woman's sage-green shawl is almost black — with blood. The black tongue, thick and stiff, pokes out of the crushed lips; her head hangs at an angle. Everything — face, neck, hands, every part of her — has turned blue-black with outraged blood. Murdered in her bed, or in her chair.

But that was not how Granny Reid died. It was not as if she, Elsie, had not been there, on the farm in the Karoo, where Granny lay in the large creaking bedstead, very still, with the fig tree pressing its midsummer fullness against the window. Uncle Jack opened the window and the fresh smell of figs drifted in, lifted the room, so that the bed rocked gently as a boat. Flights of angels, that's what Uncle Jack said, flights of angels rocking Granny to her rest. She thought of plump figs fitted with cellophane wings and gold piping.

The men in their family are large, tall as trees. With Granny dead — in her bed or on a kitchen chair, who would know — they stood about awkwardly, then gravitated towards the dining-room table just as if she had called out that lunch was ready. They folded their bodies like Swiss knives onto the chairs, snapping their knees like blades under the table.

The end of an era, Uncle Jack sighed.

Father passed him the bottle of Oudemeester, Have a *dop* man; we all need a *dop*.

No one noticed Elsie pressed against the wall.

In this hour of darkness, said Uncle Jack ponderously, steering the bottle along the edge of the crocheted doily, almost half-way round the table and back again. So that her father said, *Ag* no man, don't you start now, leave that kind of talk for Dominee. Her father, the eldest, was losing his faith. Jack sensed from the set of his shoulders that something solid was loosening, slipping. He looked to Tom for help, but Tom, the youngest and largest of the brothers, tightly wedged in his chair, sloshed brandy round and round in the tumbler, his eyes fixed on the liquid lurching from side to side.

Her father spoke in a strange, bitter voice. This country — it's all over. Gone to the dogs. The Groenewalds murdered in broad daylight and now Mamma dead in her bed.

Uncle Tom caressed his brow thoughtfully, as if he were counting brand-new furrows. Perhaps his head was aching.

Mamma died of old age, he said wearily. You know that. Arthritis, crumbling bones, rheumatism, dicky heart: all the things that anybody collects over the years. Anybody, in any country.

Believe that if you like, her father said. Who's been living here, looking after Mamma, with you lot in Town? Mamma just gave up with these bladdy elections. After the years of terrorism, just more of the same, only now of course it's all legal. Even homosexuals. Anyone in his right mind would just pack up, pack in this whole thing and start again in another place, somewhere civilised. I mean, I always said that the Nationalists went too far, looking for trouble with the politics business, so now what do we get? The opposite — people just going crazy, just wanting stuff, just wanting more and more, so it's violence everywhere. We Reids have never supported apartheid ...

Oh no? Uncle Tom interjected with a snort. No, we sure didn't have a dicky bird to do with it.

As I was saying, what use is that now that we'll all be murdered in our beds, her father continued.

Uncle Tom shook his head, then banged his fist on the table, so that the brandy slopped over the rim of his full glass. He wagged his finger as he spoke about being responsible for the mess. Elsie had heard it all before; now her father would brood and bustle with bad temper for days, storming from room to room, so that no corner of the house could escape his foul odour.

A thirteen-year-old in a fig tree, that's ridiculous, her father said. But yes, that was where Elsie hid from them all, wearing her green dungarees for camouflage. Miss Smith patted Annie's head during the lunch-break and said that all would come right, that that was how some people were when their grannies died. Elsie didn't like the idea of breaking her best friend's heart but what could she do; it had become impossible to say anything, even to Annie. There was no bolt on the door of her room, so after school she sat for hours in the fig tree. From time to time she heard the plump fruits, betrayed by their own weight, drop to the ground. Jafta whistled as he staggered up to the kitchen door with a wheelbarrow of logs; the dog had given up barking at the tree. As Jafta returned he would say, Phew, what a stink. I'm going to clean up all that rotten fruit under the tree. Thankfully, he didn't get round to it. The magic ring of fermenting fruit with its black halo of insects kept others away, kept her safely in the tree. From there she could look into Granny's room at the folded linen stacked on the mattress, at the ornate old dressing table stripped of its knick-knacks. But before you could say Jack Robinson, it was time, the cat and dog packed off to Uncle Jack, the doors bolted, the trunks locked, and Jafta and Siena standing at the kitchen door with their black, weathered faces screwed up into puzzled smiles, for all the world like bewildered hosts waving off their guests. Annie came to say goodbye and Elsie shook hands with shoulders hunched, her eyes on her own new red shoes. She did not want Annie to see the brand-new breasts that had sprouted from all that contemplation of ripe figs in the tree. From under the tree, where the swollen fruit exploded, wafted the sweet-sour smell of compost that travelled with them like a cloud of gnats, all the way to Scotland. Where it settled in the nooks and crannies of the high old-fashioned ceilings.

Not gnats. In Scotland they are called midges. And Freddie, her brother, whom she hadn't noticed on the farm, pops up as from nowhere. Bothered by his thing grown stiff and sticky, he creeps at night out of the windowless cupboard that accommodates nothing other than a bed. The estate agent said it was an indication of how fancy the building was, a servant's room off the kitchen, with just a broad shelf along the length of the bed. He creeps into her room, and bothers her with his thing. Which is mildly interesting, repellent. His face grows red and his eyes pop, and outside the traffic drones so that waves high as houses roar down the street. Elsie hates him, which does not quite mean that she wishes him dead.

But there he was, driven, she was sure, by that stiff and sticky thing, a picture of innocence in the *Glasgow Herald*, wringing the hearts of mothers, a picture that would make even a murderer's heart melt. Or so one would have thought, but that one so thoroughly covered his tracks, that the famous Scotland Yard, smartly uniformed, could only scratch their heads. Here, in the very yard of Scotland the murderer stayed at large.

What kind of society are we, asked the *Daily Record*, and the still-new neighbours who unbarred their doors to speak condolences hung their heads in shame, for it meant that they were worse than the savages of Africa, the terrorists who would come to no good once that saint, Mandela, dies. It was nearly a year before a photograph of the man who did unmentionable things to adolescent boys before he strangled them, appeared in the paper; he had flaming red hair and paper-pale skin. Elsie understood that the hair stood for uncontrollable passions. The old Scottish blood in their own family burst forth from time to time, her father had said, and as a toddler Freddie too had bright red hair and freckles. He was talking the sad nonsense of fathers deranged with grief, for at home they had always been English, and here, she soon came to understand, that that was quite different.

Elsie was no longer to walk by the river Kelvin where terrible things could happen, not even on the stretch towards the city where the traffic of people walking their dogs kept killers at bay. Swarms of river midges nevertheless sniff out the sweet-sour smell of figs that permeate her room. They find their way through the air-tight windows to buzz about her head, find their way through the shutters. All these windows have tall wooden shutters — elegant and authentic, the estate agent called them. They fold back snugly into a recess on the deep windowsill with their decorative grooved lines on display. Not outside, as on the farm where Granny Reid herself would hobble about the house in the flame-red sunsets of the Karoo to check that they were shut. The servants could not be trusted, not any more; they would shut them alright but carelessly, often forgetting to fasten the clasps, so that the shutters would rattle eerily in the wind at night. Elsie keeps her indoor shutters shut; to protect herself against the midges, she holds her head in her hands.

Like Granny Reid, Elsie wears her sage-green shawl all year round. The Glasgow summers are no warmer than the winters; only a line of heat haze hangs above the summer tourist traffic inching its way along the Great Western Road. Her father had brought the shawl from the Barras, and after polishing his brass, he washed it by hand and dried it on the pulley pressed high against the kitchen ceiling. Together they watched the shawl splayed out on the drying rack for all the world as if Granny Reid were there in Glasgow, trying to fly. It dripped onto the lino, and he rushed to mop up the drops of blood. Then the shawl disappeared and Elsie, snooping in her father's room, found it scrunched up in a cupboard. Did he wear it wrapped around his shoulders in the privacy of his room? She didn't care. Granny's sage-green shawl was not meant for a man; it belonged to her. Tonight she needs it since the black satin frock from the Oxfam shop with rhinestones around the neckline is sleeveless and virtually backless. Never before has she worn such an uncomfortable garment. Her arms are covered in goose bumps in spite of the shawl.

Elsie checks the sluggish kitchen clock. It's nearly twenty to eight. She goes around the flat once more to

133

check the doors. The sound of the wind is deafening. Will she hear the doorbell above that din? The tall boy in upper-sixth with the halting speech has asked her to the end-of-year dance. A refugee from Eritrea, she thinks he is. And the invitation perhaps a dare issued by boys with stiffly spiked hair? Hassan or Hussein, she is not sure of his name. Will he wear a kilt? They say that that is what the boys wear for the dance. There could have been some pleasure in rising, smoothing the skirt of her satin frock, and saying to her father, Ah, that will be Hassan or Hussein at the door. But her father has not remembered; he'll be at McGinty's playing darts as he does every Friday night. She thinks he has taken to drink.

When the bell rings at precisely twenty to eight Elsie scrambles into her bed, black frock and all, and pulls the covers over her head. The wind roars through the out-buildings, tearing figs from the tree, and the rain beats down so that waves high as houses leap over the slate roofs. An ark, light as a paper boat, drifts down the Great Western Road with the sail of Granny Reid's sage-green shawl flapping in the distance.

Raising The Tone

Miriam yawns, stretches, and chucks her pencil across the table.

Boring, boring, boring.

Then, remembering Babylon, she leaps on to the bed, arms flung out dramatically, and mimics, stuttering aloud, I am a B-b-british object, before collapsing and burying her face in the pillow. What a fine start that is to a story, and with so many examples of fine stories in the world, why, oh why can she not get started. Even her own story would do. Everyone should be able to think herself as the subject of a narrative, and with a trumpeting opening line like that. Except, it should be revised at the beginning of every year, otherwise people would end up like her mother — stuck in history. And a concrete pipe springs to mind, with half the old girl's body, her torso, wriggled free, but alas, the full hips unable to move any further. Stuck. Thus, unable to think herself into a different story, it is always the same opening line, and *in medias res*, since she knows that everyone she knows, knows her story, which, far from causing embarrassment, seems to bring comfort. That's the problem with grown-ups, updating their stories ever more infrequently, until they clean forget to do so as the mortgage and shopping and clipping of garden hedges take precedence.

Miriam picks up the shopping list that Cath has slipped under her door. Everything about her mother is irritating, just look at that handwriting — pathetic, like a child's. Even a shopping list can't escape the palimpsest of the old story of Africa: walking barefoot the five miles to school: and the well-worn keywords of *mieliepap, vel-skoen, sjambok,* police dogs... etcetera, etcetera. If only Miriam could move out today; it wouldn't take more than an hour to fling her few things in a bag. But first things first, a poignant opening line is all she asks for.

No need to write down these, the only words that spring to mind: I am the subject of history. So disappointing — she could flagellate herself — so transparently a product of her class in Postcolonial Writing, which she took only because of her mother's pleading. However, let it now be known that all that compliance is a thing of the past. No wonder she can't squeeze out as much as a decent opening line. The time has come for taking control of her life, of her own education. Overrated, that's what Princess Anne had to say about a university education, and while Miriam hates the idea of sharing a view with such a person, she has to agree. In fact, she can do better, for unlike the princess she has the experience of nearly two years under her belt. University stifles creativity, and in that sense it is underrated. People like her mother think of it as an escalator to the middle-classes, a means of blending in (although to *what* is never voiced), the passport to better paid jobs; they fail to appreciate its more subtle functions of knocking the stuffing out of eager youth through the ventriloquy of writing essays, the deadening effect of deadlines and timetables — all in the interest of a stable, unchallenged society, of youth drilled into submission. Not for Miriam, thank you very much; she will not be going back to finish the degree. It may well take time to throw off the bad habits of two long years, but then, who knows what she'd come up with, for sure as eggs is eggs she plans to come up with something original, something startling and creative.

Sure as eggs? Steering a shopping trolley, Miriam has just come to the end of the aisle of biscuits and crap cakes, and there, directly before her is the stand of eggs, an omen to seal her resolve. Lidl is pretty good as far as supermarkets go. The Third World shop, Mrs Dalhousie called it when it first opened, by which she meant that it is overrun with immigrants – Eastern European Gypsies, Zimbabwean asylum seekers and such – whilst she hastily added that she doesn't mean anything by that. Then Miriam said that it must have been such a person who only a month ago, at one of the Sighthill tower blocks, had been killed by his good neighbours, fellow Lidl shoppers, but the woman brushed it aside.

Och, there's no difference between folk the world over, AnnMarie Dalhousie, who had never set foot outside Glasgow claimed, except, there's no point in being careless: in Lidl you do have to keep a close eye on your handbag.

You'd swear the woman's had a university education. Well, Miriam doesn't have a handbag; instead, her mother's purse lies at the bottom of her hessian bag, and that's another good thing about Lidl — no plastic bags wantonly supplied. She grabs the eggs and heads off for the treasure trove of the central aisle full of crazy, unexpected things like riding crops, sewing kits, floral Wellington boots, mosquito nets, stuff for DIY men on the other side, and today a selection of fruit trees. Where on earth would the inhabitants of high-rise flats plant them? Besides, nectarines surely would refuse to grow on the banks of the Clyde. On the other hand, the car park these days has a number of four-by-fours, the well-heeled feeling the pinch and descending from their own middle class ghettoes ever since *The Guardian* article that praised Lidl's low prices, organic vegetables, and fancy continental foods. Mrs Dalhousie will be pleased; she is keen on the notion of raising the social tone.

Last week Cath came back with a potted mesembryanthemum, and sickening it was to see her mother hunched over a succulent with fat greyish fingers for leaves and flowers in day-glo pink. Her cheeks were flushed with nostalgia.

All the way from Namaqualand these must have come, she wailed, yes wailed. Who knows how it'll do here.

I thought Namaqualand was dull and dry, semi-desert, with sandstorms that sting your poor bare legs, Miriam mocked. Her mother's stories never quite added up.

Oh, but then the daisies — vygies, that's what we call them — arrive in spring, miraculously covering the veld. Anyway, I would never have described it as dull, she added.

Well, I heard that they're cultivated in a greenhouse just outside Greenock, Miriam lied. So the plant's bound to die out here in the cold, and anyway it hardly looks like a daisy.

She thought it necessary, healthy, to bring her mother back to earth. And the flowers certainly looked frightened, the petals huddled into a protective spear, as if they were still stuck in a travelling crate, or had to retreat under the superior gaze of native plants.

But there was no denting Cath's delight. Not at all, she explained, that's why they're called mesembryanthemum, Greek for the opening of flowers at noon. Greek, you know, that's what we Griquas speak, and she giggled in her high-pitched voice that Miriam has come to label African.

For all this sentimental nonsense the succulent at least was better than the dreadful flowers made out of coloured telephone wire that Cath brings back from home, as she still calls the Cape. Their flat is cluttered with ethnic artefacts — the rubbish drawings in felt-tip pen, rusting little bicycles and carts made out of wire, weird things with bottle tops, corks and bits of glass that her mother loves, and beadwork everywhere. Why would anyone want to cover a gourd with beads? Christ, did those people not learn anything from history? from the exchange of beads and buttons for land? It's enough to make you want to shoot them all over again.

So, why do you want to leave home Miriam? To that question she could truthfully answer that she's been driven out by beadwork.

Other than a job-lot of Greek foods nearing their sell-by date and indeterminate kids' stuff, there is nothing unusual in the central aisle today. Miriam imagines that there is a Mr Lidl, well, more likely a natty Mr Rab Liddell who, after years of bargaining, still brims with enthusiasm for shopping. On the crack of dawn Easyjet flights to Berlin, Amsterdam, or Stockholm to pick over the bargains for turning his shop into a bazaar, a real market where midst the Babel of voices the old and young, Brits and immigrants alike, can pore over the unexpected, marvel at the exotica. Here the local old biddies dragging tartan shopping trollies will nudge a black woman in a towering headdress, or a blonde girl who turns out to speak with a heavy accent: Say hen, what do you make of this? Or, holding up a knobbly celeriac: how do you eat them things? Miriam loves Lidl for being the very opposite of university; this is where she belongs, amongst ordinary people struggling to make ends meet, who delight in the cheap merchandise, even if they struggle with the new, with the weekly challenges posed by Mr Lidl, whose contempt for Tesco is palpable in the very layout of these aisles.

For all her mother's revolutionary credentials, they live in the liminal zone where their modest tenements butt on to fancy town-house terraces on the eastern side, whilst on the west, just over the road, is the working-class estate where six high-rise blocks lean precariously against grey skies. The tenements aspire to the middle-class condition of the terraces. It makes Miriam sick: middle of the road, cautious and quiet, fearful of attention and equally fearful of being overlooked, sitting tight in the middle lane of the motorway, hesitating, hedging their bets, fearful of being called upon to declare themselves, of declaring their opening sentences. People like Mrs Dalhousie (Please call me AnnMarie? Like hell she will) out of whose painted mouth came words like Pakis, Gypsies, Jewesses, and them asylum seekers who swamp the high rise where she lives. Not decent folk like youse who speak proper, she said on meeting Miriam's mother a year or more ago. Surely Cath must know that before she had been heard speaking-proper, she too was one of those darkies against whom the beleaguered natives must protect their handbags. Does her mother have no pride?

Miriam keeps out of the woman's way, rushes past the living room where Dalhousie is even allowed to smoke, and where, not so long ago she overheard the old bag consoling herself that things are looking up, that new people are raising the tone in the Burnside flats. Miriam can only assume that their car park must be boasting a couple of four-by-fours. But Cath, who these days seems to have lost her marbles, says that AnnMarie has a heart of gold. They are thick as thieves, and Miriam has recently heard her mother come in at six in the morning, which has something to do with Dalhousie, she has let on. But Miriam makes a point of not asking any questions. She keeps out of their way; they disgust her.

Cath teaches a class in childcare at the community centre where AnnMarie brings the grandchild that had been dumped on her. The child is an overgrown, bald, lard-coloured baby whose tiny features squat timidly in the centre of a fat face that grows directly out of its chest and spills over either side of an expensive pram, but Miriam is not allowed to say that. Angel child, her mother calls it.

See how that baby's transformed AnnMarie's life, has brought her close to the other people in the flats. Really, the wee sweetheart has broadened her world, made her see things quite differently.

Well, don't imagine that I'll baby sit for Mrs Raise-the-tone, Miriam warned, but Cath was sniffy. Oh, no need for that at all. AnnMarie's got an amazing system in place, across all the blocks on the estate. Those people are on the ball, really well organised.

For hours, Miriam sits at the table overlooking the street. Now that she's resolved not to return to uni, she really must try harder. But her page as usual is blank. The only progress she has made today is to prevent herself from doodling in the margins. If no words, then neither squiggles, nor any movement: that's her new motto. Which means that her eyes are fixed on the tenements over the road, since being stuck here at the table gives her licence to stare across at the matching first floor flat into the neighbours' rooms. She may not know the McFarlanes, but she certainly knows their habits: the couple's silent breakfasts in the mornings; the ritual watering of window boxes before they go off to work, in spite of the daily summer rain; the man's return at five-thirty when he walks about swigging from a beer bottle. At night Miriam can follow through a lit bathroom window the silhouette of the woman lowering herself on to the toilet. Such sad faith in frosted glass, or do the McFarlanes know that they can be seen? Miriam is transfixed by the shape shifting, the bent form of elbows resting on thighs until the woman rises, with a sigh perhaps? Twisting into her pants and turning to fasten a zip. Then there is the man, who turns his back, jiggles his shoulders, bends slightly to unzip, and Miriam watches as he finishes, straightens up, and adjusts his clothes. Sure as eggs, there'll be piss on the floor, a drop or two on the seat – that's what men do, even as guests in other people's houses, as if they have never been told that that poor design requires scrutiny after the act. Thank God there are no men in their house. The very thought makes her gag.

Miriam is nearly nineteen and sick to death of life. Christ, she could so easily take a razor to her throat. Searing pain, how much better that than this steady dum-dum-dum that passes for a heartbeat, this dreary, stultifying, stifling, boring, boring, boring...

Cath is only mildly alarmed. You'll regret it, she says.

It obviously won't be easy to top myself; there wouldn't be any point, would there, if it were easy, but what I really can't do is regret it afterwards. There won't be a me, a sentient subject, I mean a sentient being, to feel regret.

Cath sighs. She means leaving university before finishing the degree, rather than nonsense about topping herself.

Well, that too takes courage, Miriam says. What she yearns for is to take control of her own life, but she has been through this conversation before and with no new arguments, no new entailments, she would rather not go into all that again. Best to avoid repetition, the mouldy story of her mother's years in The Struggle, the predictable lament: Where I come from children respect their elders, appreciate their parents' efforts, not the cheeky, pampered creatures... But Cath too seems to have lost interest. She sits on the sofa staring distractedly at the beaded Zulu blanket; her dejection appears to have nothing to do with their argument, so that Miriam asks, What's up? Without taking her eyes off the blanket, her mother says mildly, flicking her wrist, Oh, off you go. Nothing you'd be interested in, nothing you wouldn't call the old African story.

Dismissed like a kid. Miriam walks straight out the front door without picking up her keys. It is mild, and a walk might do her good, might clear her head for writing. She crosses the main road to the estate of high rise flats where the grounds are inviting, generously landscaped into sweeping hillocks and mini vales, with clumps of mature trees that turn it into something of a park. She might even write something set in that park. Ahead, there is a playground with swings and slides and roundabouts where a group of women in salwar kameezes stand gathered around shrieking children. If she keeps away from the playground there should be no danger of running into anyone she knows.

The lawns have just been mown, and the sweet smell of cut grass goes some way towards making up for the dilapidated buildings, incongruous in that lovely setting. Then the sun comes bursting out. Light bounces off gilded window panes so that it is difficult to count the floors, but Miriam does so twice, until she is sure that there are eighteen. Testament to the utopian vision of the sixties, the tower blocks, built for shipyard workers she supposes, stand at various angles to each other, once proud in the landscaped grounds. They all have names, conjuring up the Scottish romance of lochs and mountains, but a number of the letters have fallen off, so that it is a matter of guessing. According to AnnMarie's old story it was bionic, bouffant-headed Thatcher who in the eighties, with no voters in Glasgow, took revenge by killing off ship-building. So the original workers packed their bags and left in droves, hence the asylum seekers who are bussed into places like these, pegged into estates where natives have left holes.

Miriam is blinded by forked spears of light from a glass panel, a Blakean moment that announces her future. This is where she should live, in a cheap, council flat. If there is room for immigrants, why not a little flat for her? It would be amazing on the top floor where you'd have a magnificent view of the city. If it were not a Sunday, she would go to the Housing Office right now to check out the possibility. In the meantime, she will nose about the nearest block, perhaps take the lift to the top floor.

At the base of the tower LO–ON– that has lost its M and D each steel-rimmed panel below the ground floor windows is entirely covered with paintings. These are clearly the works of foreigners: stylized landscapes with weird flora; seascapes with strange oriental-looking boats; an exotic black woman whose elaborate headdress has taken over, expanded into abstract patterns that fill the entire frame; a copy of one of Hokusai's Mount Fuji views. In each the handling of paint is different. Miriam lingers before the ones that look like frescoes, where the pigment seems to have seeped into the concrete. The same painter, she imagines. How on earth had the artist managed to make his mark in the very fabric of the building? A bold gesture, speaking as much as longing for another place, as inserting himself here in Glasgow into the history of LO–ON–. Her head fizzes with excitement.

This is a place where people are alive, where new things are thought and done, where she could get involved.

When a man in green overalls comes through the double doors, she slips in and hurriedly makes for the lift. A group of people follow her; a family of parents and four children crowd into the lift. The children press up against her, and the smell of alcohol and pee makes her stomach heave. The woman, who has no top teeth, says something that Miriam doesn't understand, but she nods her head vigorously and smiles. As they leave the lift, the man, also afflicted with a speech impediment addresses her. Fockin' this and fockin' that, he hisses through blackened stumps of teeth; his manner is hostile; he seems to hold her responsible for something or other. Loony, for sure, or perhaps he takes her for an asylum seeker. She is relieved when the happy family shuffle off at the tenth floor. God forbid that she should ever reproduce herself.

Miriam notes the surveillance camera in the top corner of what otherwise is a continuous gleaming surface of textured aluminium panels, the only area that's been refurbished. On the eighteenth floor the lift shudders to a halt and she slips out furtively. The landings on either side are run-down spaces: cracked grey tiles mark out the edges of the floor, the rest having been worn down by years of foot-treads into concrete depressions where leaked water stagnates. At the end of each landing from where a balcony can be accessed is a door to the top flat. What will she do if someone were to open the door — Yes, what do you want? The camera would after all have spied her and who knows, a message may already be circulating through the building, her image reproduced in each flat. She is not sure how these cameras work, or who they are accountable to.

Moira Finnegan: that is the name that springs to mind, the opinionated girl in her tutorial group. That is what she'll say, that she's looking for Moira Finnegan, a friend who has recently moved to the top floor of these flats, although she can't remember which block it is. Moira was the one that sucked up to the mealy-mouthed tutor, a research student who taught the class whilst the professors did who knows what behind closed doors. Clear as daylight she sees from these heights a fresh life without tutorials unfold before her.

Miriam steps out on to the balcony on the west side. What an amazing view, and yes, she would certainly be happy living here. Through the tops of huge old oak trees a silver sliver of river gleams through the disused shipyards, and beyond lie the distant hills or mountains that would have inspired the names of these flats. For all the dilapidation of the building — she kicks against the rusted railings — the grounds below are bright and spacious, with all the magic that an aerial view bestows. Even the abominable cars are grand, parked in paved arcs that look like giant commas punctuating the green. From up here one can see back in time to the architect's drawing board, his vision revealed, realised in the paths and buildings set in a park. Under a bower of trees beside the next building — Miriam cannot read the name of the mountain although it would seem as if all the letters are in place — a family in bright colours is picnicking under grey skies, for the sun has once again disappeared. There are surveillance cameras all along the pathways, but it is good that people go about their business regardless, undeterred by these fascistic measures.

In this park she would be able to think clearly, sitting on the bench under a copper beech, away from the sterility of Holyrood Street with its shaved privet hedges and lack of garden. How odd that the tenements should be considered more desirable than these flats. Here Miriam would meet different kinds of folk, people with whom to discuss the paintings at the base of the buildings. No need for them to find definitive opening lines; there are the living images, expression of raw feeling and desire. There is the very building on whose walls the paintings are executed represented within the paintings, although always with a buttery, beaming sun, and the clichés of doves circling the tower, no doubt in response to the toothless snarls of the natives. How interesting it would be to have a real community, people with whom to talk about the ins and outs of such pictures. Perhaps, she, Miriam, should think of taking up painting herself; after all she had achieved a B for her Higher in Art in spite of her contempt for the moustachioed teacher whose name she refuses to remember.

A door creaks and children tumble noisily out of the top floor flat, accompanied by a woman's tired voice. No, no dinnae youse start playing up. Give it him back Mary. Now. I said, Now.

Miriam imagines that they are too preoccupied to give her the once over. She stands stock still with her back to them. Better to pretend that she belongs there, but when she hears the lift shaft creak, she too goes down. Below in the foyer are a group of men speaking in a language she doesn't know; they do not look like artists.

Cath is in the sitting room listening to a five o'clock news bulletin. If Miriam is not mistaken, her face is damp with hastily wiped tears. What's up, she says briskly; her mother's sentimentality must not be encouraged. Then it comes to her in a flash: the menopause, yes, that would explain the past couple of days. You should see a doctor, she adds, sinking into a chair. Cath will know how you go about getting yourself on the council's housing list, that is, if she can be distracted from the dated soap opera that is her life.

Cath presses the remote control listlessly. Enough of this, she sighs, God knows where it will all end. Who would have thought that after apartheid people would turn to such brutality against fellow Africans? Christ, is this what we fought for?

Uh-huh? Miriam says.

Haven't you heard about the migrants from the north being persecuted, killed by people in Gauteng?

As it happens, yes, Miriam had seen the news and the

commentary last night. Well, she explains, the government just hasn't delivered its promises; people are as poor as ever, and they see these Zimbabweans and Nigerians as a further drain on...

Cath interrupts, impatient. Yes, of course there are some sectors where little has changed, but what to do now? Today? How to prevent the poor from sinking into further degradation, inflicting further misery on to their fellow sufferers and of course themselves? I know there's no comparison, but just look at the Burnside estate across the road here...

It is Miriam's turn to interrupt. She can't believe her luck, her mother introducing the tower blocks herself. I was going to ask you, she says, about the estate, about the chances of getting a flat, sharing one if necessary. How do you get yourself on to the council's list? Do you know what the waiting list looks like?

Cath leaps to her feet. Do you have no sense of decency? No thought for anyone other than yourself? There's history being made before your very eyes and all you can think of is your own precious personal arrangements.

Miriam should have known that the calm, liberal acquiescence about her leaving home was all talk. Clearly her mother resents her plans to leave. Probably can't face living alone. No one on whom to dump the old stories of her days as a resistance fighter. She gives Cath a pitying glance as she leaves the room.

***

Miriam looks at the clock. It is five a.m. She has just been woken up she thinks by sirens, fire engines most likely, since this city seems to be a haven for pyromaniacs. Then, on her way to the lavatory, the telephone in the hall rings. Cath, a voice shouts hoarsely, I've sent the Hukkars round to you. Then the line goes dead.

Cath is up, struggling into her dressing gown. Is it AnnMarie? she asks, Another bloody dawn raid? No

147

sooner has she turned on the kettle than the doorbell rings.

The people at the door are drenched, and in various states of undress. There are three children, and from Mrs Hukkar's torn jacket, worn over lime green pyjamas, juts a prickly twig of flowering hawthorn.

An-an-anMa sa-said to come to you, Mr Hukkar stutters. His face is drawn.

Yes, of course, Cath says, ushering them in.

Miriam, who has pulled a kagoul over her pyjamas, now pulls the hood over her head. What else can she do but pretend that she knows what's going on: the raids by immigration officers trying to arrest asylum seekers; the daily dawn patrols at Burnside, organised by AnnMarie to thwart them; and the telephonic alarm system that warns the immigrants to seek refuge with assigned neighbours. But this time, Mrs Hukkar explains, the police are intent on raiding all the flats, Scots and all, and AnnMarie thought it best to send families out of the building, down the fire stairs. She said she'd come over to Cath's afterwards.

Cath laughs. Oh, AnnMarie will want to see the whole raid through to the end; she loves getting the crowd to stand outside and jeer at the immigration people as they leave the building empty-handed. That's all part of the reward, so last time I showed them how to *toyi-toyi* African style. How we flummoxed those guys, hey? With arms akimbo and her bum stuck out, Cath starts stomping about the room, ululating a resistance cry.

K-k-k quite so, Mr Hukkar says politely, taking coffee from the tray that Miriam hands round. It is clear that he cannot be persuaded to join in, but two of the children are stomping along. The younger, having grabbed the beaded gourd from the side-board, trumpets into it, Nee-naw, Nee-naw, after the police cars, and quite drowns Cath's Xhosa song.

N2

They argued all the way from Stellenbosch.

Something odd, as they sat around the table toasting Jaap's prize-winning pinot noir — later she thought of a spiked drink — slipped into what she had described to her girlfriends as a nice 'n' easy relationship. A lovely evening it was too, with the mountain just taking colour, and in her hand the crystal flute with those divine little beads jostling at the brim.

Now for this barbarian, she had smiled into Jaap's sunburnt face, you must fill it right up, almost to the brim, yes, just so, so I can watch the suicide leap of the bubbles. No half-glass for me.

As a child Mary loved weddings. Then grown-ups sipped from wide-brimmed coupes at darling little ponds of champagne. She supposed it hadn't been real but what did she care about such snobbish distinctions, *methode champenoise* sounded grand enough for her; it was the effervescence that counted. She watched the sparkles rising from the bottom in a stream of light and bubble at the brim. Oh, there was nothing like it, bubbles that hurled themselves at her, that couldn't wait to be taken. That's what's best, the moment before, when for seconds you are queen of a world of pleasure that awaits. Mary saw herself fixed in a photograph, with glass held to lips moist with expectation, chin — still young and firm — regally lifted, but there you are, who can resist greed, even when you know that that moment is best, that the actual thing falls just short of its promise. Like sex, she supposed, and surprised herself by casting a resentful look across the table at Harold.

Harold, only half-focused on the still-life of crystal, liquor and lips, was asking about vines cultivated on higher slopes, about the heavy sandstone loams, and so caught that ugly look with puzzlement. Was she bored? Uncomfortable about something or other? Not that her demand for a full-to-the-brim flute was not charming. He had half-smiled, solicitously. No wonder she felt cross, not knowing what to make of such a hybrid look.

Yes, sex. She would have liked to have said it out loud. That's what people like Harold with all their talk of politics don't think of, that there are now all kinds of freedoms. Just think, that a man who had sat in prison for decades, no champagne, no sex, was the one to push the country into the twentieth century, into the civilised world; she had been to Amsterdam where they made no bones about these things. Now everyone here at home could talk about it, see it on television, read about it in magazines, even in poems. No need any longer for men to make sinful trips to the Wild Coast or Sun City, it was all there to be had at home. And what's more, for women as well. Sex between all kinds, although she would have drawn the line there, perhaps taken one step at a time, no good being too advanced, even stepping ahead of England, but that's freedom for you, just as De Klerk said, freedom is unstoppable.

All of which prolonged the moment of anticipation, for the glass was still held to her mouth while she pondered liberation, until Harold, now attentive, watched the composition come to life: the glass pressed against cherry-red lips parted, the liquor spurting. Behind her, the sun was dipping fast, drunkenly, in the usual gold and reds, and then the light, how the light ricocheted from the crystal as she tilted it to her lips. The *something* flare of lightning ... beaded bubbles *something* at the brim ... Mary thought of lines that were once, perhaps, recited at school; she couldn't quite remember.

150

It was getting late. From below in Idas Valley the smell of location woodsmoke rose, and the *skelbek* of a drunk woman could be heard above the distant beat of *kwela* music. It was time they went home.

Drink up, said Harold, still smiling. Only one glass for him; he was driving. Jaap pushed a bottle across the table. To lay down.

Ag, no man, what's the use of a prize-winner if you can't pass it round?

And again, Drringcupp. Crass like the *skelbek* that drifted onto the terrace, his voice cut through the first sifting of frangipani as the light drained quickly, helter-skeltering after an already-sunken sun.

She turned to Jaap. What a beauty you have here — has she said that before? — top marks from me.

Oh, I can't take all the credit. I've got some first-class men working for me. My manager, he can tell just the right moment to irrigate, that's crucial you see, and I've even got a chap here from Idas Valley who knows every-thing there is to know about *hanepoot*.

He smiled, shyly for such a big man who stretched com-fortably, brown arms flung out as if blessing the table. But the table too had had it. Others had left their traces on crumpled napkins; the cloth was stained with wine; and beside the posy of wild flowers an oyster canapé lay capsized, its crushed stern flung to the edge, to the printed border of guinea-fowl craning their speckled necks onto the table. Mary folded her napkin, placed it over the scrap of pastry. Post-prandial sadness flitted across her face.

Time we went, Harold announced in a first-time voice.

Ah, she thought, a spike of jealousy. That's what it was, jealous of Jaap who travelled to Europe once, twice a year with his estate wines. And oh yes, what if she were not ready to go, what if she did not think it time? But coming as it did, belatedly, the thought slunk off. So she looked deep into the empty glass, spun the stem, set it down, and pinged with her perfect nail against the crystal. Which made the men rise. Their chairs scraped against the stone paving of the terrace.

Ja-nee, said Jaap, that motorway is no joke in the dark. I see those squatter people have started throwing stones from the bridge again, something in this morning's *Cape Times* about the N2. *Kapaah!* he beat together his large hands. Also onto a Merc it was, but on the other side, coming from Cape Town. Luckily it hit the back.

Mary thought of the three wild men. On the N2 that morning, as they drove to Stellenbosch, the black men leapt naked, except for skimpy loincloths, out of the bush, ran across the dual carriageway jumping the barriers, and disappeared into the bush on the other side. Their faces were covered in grey clay. They may have carried shields and spears.

Ag what can one do, she shrugged, there's nothing to do other than brave it out. That's now the new life for us hey, just braving it out on that chicken-run.

Jaap's *kapaah!* hands fell, See-you-soon, on her shoulders. Then she felt quite sober.

Princess's boy, the eldest, it was not that he did anything in particular, he just was funny, different from other children. Mrs Matsepe could not put her finger on it. Eh, that Themba was deep-deep, which may have made for a charming little boy, always with his head tilted asking funny questions like an old man, but now that he was no longer little, there was a strange brooding air about him that surely would bring trouble. And what can you do? — you can pray and pray to God to keep the children safe, but that's life, nothing but trouble, nothing to do, just the business of braving it out.

Funny how children grow overnight, and for that matter a boy who doesn't eat much. Even over the big days, Christmas and New Year, just like that turning fussily away from all the special food, and still shooting tall and broad into his eighteenth year, a good-looking boy with Princess's firm chin and deep-black skin, so that she wrote to her sister to say how fine he looked, never mind the strangeness that had already started to set in, she supposed, when his voice finally broke.

Princess wrote to say that yes, Themba had written,Themba now wanted to go back to school, start where he left off in Standard Six, Themba wanted to be a photographer. And in the envelope was twenty rand. Twenty rand, eh, the girl must be mad sending big notes in the post with all these *skelm* postmen who sit in the dunes with the mailbags and a tube of glue, going through people's letters before delivering them, late in the day, when the sun is already sitting in the middle of the sky. But miracle of miracles, the money slipped past the hands of those *skelms*, which is something to be thankful for, and another thing, at least Themba didn't want to be a postman.

But still, Mrs Matsepe was hurt. The boy was her own since so-so high, since before she herself had children. Why had he not spoken to her? If only she had thought of it first, that he should go back to school, that they could manage again now that things were getting better. But Jim said, and Jim too was no less than his father, Jim said it was only right, it was only respectful that he should write to Princess first, that he appreciated having two mamas, that he should test out his ideas on paper before blurting out things that might come out wrongly. That was when she stopped listening. Having given her this bullshit wisdom he would in any case expect her to speak to Themba. Which was just as well. Only last week, when she complained about the boy's strangeness, Jim of all people came up with such a kaffir-idea that she just had to shake her head.

About this Themba business, he said, I thi-ink ... and then stared deeply into his mug as if she had nothing better to do than stand around waiting. As if she were not about to take her life in her hands as she did every morning before sunrise, squash herself into a show-off taxi that would hurl itself recklessly all over the N2, as if driving people under cover of pounding music into a death of steel and fire were better than delivering them to their places of work. Not for Mrs Matsepe — she adjusted her beret — that was her name, that's who she was, since the day she decided to hell with laws and in-laws and came to the city after Jim, her lawfully-wedded husband. No, after all those troubles — and now also Jim with a head full of foolish ideas — she would survive any taxi-ride to get to her Greenoaks Nursing Home, where she was in charge of all the cleaning girls. No, for her it was nice to get out to Rosebank every day, nice to be spread out amongst trees and purple flowering bushes, away from the noise of the motorway, from the filth of Crossroads. She would not give up hope that they'd get away; it was just a matter of time.

Jim cleared his throat to continue, but then the blue work van hooted, and without grabbing his lunch-pack he rushed off. So now he'd have to spend money on slap-chips. It was she, Mrs Matsepe, who got up early, got everyone ready for the day, packed his bread with peanut butter and a nice sprig of parsley she took from the Greenoaks garden. She admired the way cook put a curly bit of green on the dinner plates, made everything so nice and appetising, but that man of hers was too stupid. It was not till night-time, in the creaking bed, whispering so as not to wake the children, and worried about Themba who was not yet home, it was not till then, and with an elbow nudge from her, that he returned to his thought.

Themba must go to the bush, to initiation, it's the right way to turn him into a man, help him over this difficult business of growing up. He must go into the bush.

She could tell from his voice that his heart wasn't in it, but still, she really didn't expect such a backward idea from a Christian man. What could have got into Jim?

The bush, she exploded, call that strip along the N2 a bush? Just a rubbish scrap of trees left there to keep our place out of sight.

Yes, but it's still our bush, that's what we've made of it; we must make do, it's all we have for the young ones to go to, to become men. Even the students have started going to the bush ...

As if that meant anything, Mrs Matsepe snorted. Those students were *toyi-toying* fools, always going on strike, loafing about at weekends, doing those terrible things to girls in the hostels and then talking rubbish about roots and traditional culture. She supposed that that was what Themba wanted to be, a student.

I'm saying to you now and I won't say it again, Jim. No people of mine are going to have anything to do with such backward things. A pretend-bush in Town, that's the very last I want to hear of it.

But now, with Themba back at school, now a young man, who carried on scowling and shrugging his shoulders and going about with others who looked as if they carried guns, she did not know what to think. What if she were wrong? If it were the only way to pull him right, should she not think again about initiation? If the boy himself were to ask, would she not say, yes anything?

But Themba said nothing. Themba did not speak; he sat with his head buried in books.

For a few seconds before he braked sharply, the car hobbled as if the road had grown potholed. Mary raised her eyebrows and turned away disdainfully. The last straw, said her look.

So now I'm responsible for the behaviour of the car, he said.

I said nothing at all. I don't care who's responsible, but I would like to get back to civilisation. This is no place to get stuck in the dark.

We're not stuck, he hissed. Then, resolving to be patient, it was after all no joke for a woman to find herself in the middle of nowhere: It won't take a minute, just a puncture, just a matter of changing the wheel. I got the spare checked just the other day.

155

He opened his door a fraction, and in the light leant over her to scrabble in the cubby hole for a torch. Mary shrank into the corner, her head turned to look into the moonless night.

Themba heard the screech of the car coming to a halt just yards away. He had made himself a hide-out in the Port Jackson bushes, had cleared the space of rubbish blown from the houses, and had dug out with his hands something of a dip in which to settle himself comfortably. Here he often sat in the dark, with the smell of earth not quite smothered by petrol fumes, the sound of the traffic a steady whoosh and hum, and through the screen of reeds and bushes his eyes followed the flashes of light and the sleek shapes of cars sailing by in the black night. Behind him, Crossroads was drowned in darkness.

Themba sat up, squatting to see the yellow light spill onto the shoulder of the road, the light on the woman's cropped yellow head. He watched the man wrenching at the handbrake, swinging his long legs out onto the tarmac and, in another pool of propped torchlight, opening the boot and lifting out a jack. Themba could see that he hasn't done this before, not on the chassis of this car. The man groped for a place to fit the jack, looked about ruefully for a second, then slid on his back under the belly of the car, a silver beauty of a Mercedes Benz ... yes he'd found it, the jackpoint. Now he reached for the wheel brace to loosen off the nuts.

In the intimate interior of the car the woman's yellow head was bent over a handbag in which she pushed things about, groping for something at the bottom. Another flash of light within that lit space, then a glowing circle of red as she drew deeply from a cigarette. She stared straight ahead. A car rushed past. For a second, her face shone white and still.

Fuck. Fuck. The voice cracked into the night so that Themba started, losing his balance. The man threw down the brace in a rage, then picking it up again, pushed with all his might, with clenched teeth, at the nut that would not budge. The woman's head was turned, towards the bush; she had heard a branch give as Themba toppled on tensed ankles. Oblivious to the angry grunting of the man, her hand groped in the bag, while her eyes flitted in search of the invisible branch.

Themba squirmed with guilt. For spying on them, for not helping the man. But it was not his fault that they had landed right there at his private place, displaying themselves in their own light, acting out their business in slow motion it seemed, before his eyes, and hearing Mrs Matsepe's voice to keep away from white people, to keep out of trouble, he hesitated.

Then he stood up, parted the branches noisily and walked straight out onto the road. The man's back was turned. The *mlungu* woman was out of the car in a flash, like a movie star, kicking open the door, her gun clasped in both hands was trained on him. He held up his hands, stuttered, Ho-hokaai lady, I'm just coming to help, get the wheel loose so we can put on the new one lady. Stupidly betraying himself as spy.

In slow motion the hands were lowered, a slow smile twitched on her face as she looked him in the eye, the moody boys' eyes, *ag* he was only a kid, and her lips settled, smiling, Yes, sorry, you know what it's like on the N2 ...

The man was taking the gun out of her hand, pushing it casually into his own back pocket, smiling energetically at Themba. *Ag* man, she's just a bundle of nerves, and pointing to the wheel, it's these bladdy nuts, you can have a go if you like but I've been trying all this time you know.

We must put something by the front wheel, the boy said.

Themba picked up the torch to search the ground and pointed the light at a suitable stone. A moment's hesitation before the man bent down to pick it up himself. With the front wheel wedged, he tried again and shook his head. He watched the boy straining against the brace. Just his luck that the boy should be the one to shift the nuts.

157

I think, said Themba, as if he hadn't managed it, they'll perhaps come loose under the jack. Together they pushed aside the clutter in the boot, the toolbag, an old rug and what looked like a brand-new Nikon camera, shifted these to lift out the spare, and in a jiffy the car was jacked up, the old wheel off, the new one fixed.

Themba was wiping his hands on his trousers as they got into the car. The windows rolled down simultaneously. Together they spoke their scrambled words of thanks, then her voice above his, laughing, It's so good of you I don't know what... and the man's, Yes, that was a devil of a wheel, thank you man, and one day I'll be the one to roll a stone out of your path hey.

Again the noise as their voices merged, and the key turned and the Merc started up, and it was as if from a distance, joining the gibberish of thanks, that he heard a thin sound coming from an unknown place inside and distinctly the words, Please sir, madam, have you please got some rands? Then the scramble in pockets, in the handbag, and two sets of white hands dropped the notes — Yes of course, *ag* shame man, sorry we just weren't thinking — into the bowl of his very own prosthetic hands.

His hands were on fire. Themba stuffed a burning note into each of his pockets, felt the fire running down his legs and back up through his body, so that he sprinted home with the repetition of his own voice in tinny echo, Please sir madam have you please got some rand some rand some rand ...

Mrs Matsepe dropped her dishcloth right there on the floor and followed the boy, a streak of fire she could have sworn, into the room where the youngest was already asleep. Themba whipped the money out of his pockets, two twenty-rand notes, and threw them on the bed.

It's for you, he whispered, from the people on the road. I helped them change a wheel.

And they gave you money?

Themba dropped his eyes. Some rands, some rands, some rands, echoed in his head. He said slowly, watching his hands curve once again into a cup: I asked for the money. From *mlungu* in a Merc. I begged.

With her eyes fixed on the boy, on the face twitching with shame, Mrs Matsepe took the notes, folded them together, then tore them, carefully, into halves, into quarters, into eighths, and again, into tiny scraps of paper that she held aloft, clenched in fists, before showering them onto the bed.

In The Botanic Gardens

There were several accounts of his last movements. But she remembered only two. And the first only dimly, so that she imagined that it had been whispered by one of the other South African students, a girl called Tsiki, who held her hand and puffed continuous smoke into a small narrow room: he had been brought home by a friend who saw him to his room at 11.30 p.m. Then he disappeared.

The other was delivered by the man from the British Council, Mr MacPherson. Dorothy Brink did not quite catch his name but decided that Sir would be an appropriate form of address. The man was in national dress; he wore a green tartan kilt, a short tweed jacket and tassels on his socks. He spoke very fast, so it was difficult to follow him, but perhaps she would not have understood anyway. His English was very smart, she supposed, quite different even from the English of the SABC newsreader; he might as well have been speaking a special language understood only by those in national costume.

She tried to concentrate but could not get rid of the funny feeling that these sounds did not add up to functional words that would tell her anything about her son. She could summon up no image of Arthur whose blue aerogrammes lay in a ribbon-tied bundle in her bag. Like a lover's letters. She knew them by heart; she had read them all night long. This soft, clipped voice, claiming to follow footsteps now, twelve days later when not an echo remained, prevented her from imagining a young man called Arthur. She wanted to ask what shoes he wore, but here in Glasgow her English would squeak like crickets in a thorn-bush; besides, the man did not expect her to say anything. He had introduced her to himself: Eh, Mrs Breenk, and replied to his own enquiry after her welfare, How are you. As well as can be expected, eh.

Not that Dorothy was not grateful, but she seemed to have no control over the thickening of her tongue. If she could hear something like 'black brogues', perhaps she could understand that he was indeed speaking of Arthur, a young man who stood with her only three months ago in Bata in Kerkstraat and explained, Mamma, they're back in fashion. But these kilted words were about inaudible footsteps in a strange city where she had as yet not seen a single person in black brogues.

They sat in a room that reminded her of the in-flight film which she saw through an insistent reel of still images. Of Arthur as a toddler, in his school uniform, with the first traces of stubble, at the airport with a scholarship to Glasgow University. An elegant room, Michael Caine said from the corner of his mouth as he strode about, idly — and rudely, if you asked her, she had certainly taught her children manners right from the start — picking up an ornament before sitting down in a chintz armchair. Then Arthur as a young man, never ashamed of helping her with the housework.

She had waited by the door while her host emerged from behind his desk to shake her hand. They sat in a cluster of chintz chairs and coffee table at the far end of the room and, like Michael Caine, she looked at the high ceiling while the man in the kilt poured coffee from a glass pot with a plunger; at the cornice, elaborately moulded, and the ornate ceiling rose, an intricate pattern of spiky leaves, and she recognised the paintbrush-heads of flowering thistle. A room of muted colours in which to speak about death. The walls were a pale grey, the woodwork a shade deeper, the plush carpet another bluish grey and, looking out through the tall windows, sets of panes imposed a grid on the vast canvas of uniform grey representing a sky that spoke nothing of the weather. For by weather she understood either rain or the clear sky of Namaqualand.

She started at his movement. He placed his right leg across the other, his left hand clutching the right ankle. His eyes wandered, then came to settle just below Dorothy's left ear lobe. She dropped her eyes onto the large knee, a brutally scrubbed plain of cartilage, and resolved to concentrate. He was still speaking of the Botanic Gardens where a guard saw a young man at 11p.m. who answered to the description of Arthur and whom he recognised as someone who frequented the Kibble Palace. But why he was telling her about the huge hot-house? He had said that she should go and see the place for herself and she had nodded dutifully. But he went on:

... a lovely structure, our Kibble Palace — very old — built a long time ago on Loch Long, where it was privately owned, and then the entire glass structure was floated down the river Clyde on a raft. Brought to the Botanic Gardens in the nineteenth century. But it's unbearably hot, of course. Tropical conditions, you understand, for these marvellous plants from all over the world: Australia, South Africa, New Zealand, India and, of course, America. Absolutely marvellous, like travelling ...

Arthur wanted to travel — right round the world. Wanted to be first an engine driver, then a pilot or a ship's captain, nothing special, just dream-boasted like the other children, like Jim and little Evvie. A slight boy in short trousers and scarred knees, darker than the rest of his skin, almost black, who stuck his hands into his pockets and with the remarkable combination of lisping and rolling his 'r's, which she knew would take him far, managed to say, Sthee-e, sthee-e, when I come back with bagth full of money I'll marry Mamma and we'll have sth-weeth every day.

She shut her eyes momentarily to wrench her mind from the image of the boy and concentrated on the man's words. But he too had slipped up, had allowed his mind to wander, so that he carried on like any tourist guide.

... also the People's Palace is well worth visiting. Another glass structure, smaller, but devilishly hot too — eh, for the plants, of course. Lovely tropical things. The rest of the building is a museum — the history of the working people of Glasgow. You'll find that interesting, coming from South Africa. Very important to have these records. Of the struggle ... eh ... you'll understand how here in Scotland ... but remembering the people of the city, eh, that's what being human is all about. Aye, well worth a wee visit and not a bad place, of course, to have a bite of lunch either eh ...

He faltered as Dorothy leaned forward, frowning. How could Arthur be the subject of this talk? What was the man saying? Who was this man in the kilt? She had surely come to the right place; he had expected her, welcomed her himself. Or was he speaking in code? Arthur had once said to her after a strange telephone conversation, Don't get upset, a person can't speak plainly any more; you can't be safe without a code. *Ag*, then she let it ride; she didn't want to be bothered with such things and now, not knowing anything of politics, she was failing Arthur. A bird flapped its dark wings in her chest. Panic widened her eyes.

Mr MacPherson, whose words had strayed so wantonly, bit into a syllable then shot out a hand that hovered in the horizontal to steady her. He had seen television images of South Africans at gatherings, black women ululating and stamping their feet, and really he would not know what to do about such behaviour in the office; he would steady her with practical advice.

Mrs Breenk, you'll need distraction of this kind. This is a difficult business eh coming to terms with Arthur's eh ... but above all it is important to keep calm. The People's Palace is outwith this area but trying to find one's way is, of course, good for occupying the mind. Keep going and you'll keep in control.

As if she would lose control here amongst strange white people. Oh, she didn't understand this talk that had nothing to do with her; it was all her fault and it was no good finding out about a code now that it was all too late. She, a woman without learning, who had not managed to keep Arthur from politics, could only sit quietly and obey the hand stretched out like Dominee's with blue veins and liverish patches, commanding her to remain seated. Only when the hand dropped to the side and the knees moved and the body folded out into the vertical did she read his movements as a sign for her to rise. Her movements followed his; the navy-blue handbag, held with both hands before her, faced his sporran apologetically.

So, Mrs Breenk, as you can see, we're doing our best. But, and he paused to look at her gravely, one must realistic. It would be foolish to hold out too much hope.

She did not care about her words squeaking. In a high voice that ran like mice along the curlicues of the cornice, she said, Yes sir. No hope. I have no hope at all. But it's the body. It's, please, the body sir. I am his mother; I must see Arthur's body.

He pressed his hands together in pointed compassion. And lowered his voice. Mrs Breenk. I understand. I understand your concern but we are doing our best. We shall have to be patient but I can assure you that the police are doing their best.

Sir I would like to speak to one of the other children from home. There was a girl, Tsiki; I saw her yesterday ...

I'm afraid, Mrs Breenk, that that won't be possible. These young people — and not only the students from South Africa — have a heavy programme. An unfortunate time really. You see they're taking exams and we here at the British Council are concerned that the unfortunate disappearance of Arthur should not cause any further upset amongst our students. It's a difficult business being a student in a foreign country where you're not only contending with new ideas but also a foreign language, of course. I think you'll agree, Mrs Breenk, that further contact with the other students would be inadvisable. Young people, and especially the young women, are so vulnerable, so easily upset.

Mr MacPherson prised apart his hands for the greeting. She fumbled with the bag and transferred a scented handkerchief to her left hand in order that her right could be vigorously shaken by him.

A taxi waited to take her back to the hotel and she had to say that she was well looked after. That at least she could take back to Vlaklaagte: that the British Council provided taxi-drivers who said Yes Ma'am and drove her to a comfortable, if old-fashioned, hotel. Also, a nice young woman from the British Council had taken her to the hotel last night, even if she did go on rather foolishly about light switches: On and Off, as if she were God trying out the sun on the first day. On. See? pointing to the lampshade suspended from a high-as-heaven ceiling and: Off, with a voice inflected for darkness. Quite ridiculous and funny how it made her think of the oil lamps of the early days. Arthur was the one who could not bear a smudge of smoke on the lamp glass; he kept it sparkling. Always particular, her Arthur who loved his Mamma, she assured herself, loved his Mamma for sure, but the girl asked if she wanted to try for herself? On. Off. She shook her head. Whatever would these people say next? Still, it had been easy enough to understand the girl who said, as if she could read her thoughts, If you prefer to eat alone here in your room, just telephone down and order something and don't worry about money. The British Council will see to everything. She wished she had asked Arthur what this British Council business was; she had hoped to ask one of the other students.

Dorothy eased herself onto the bed still holding her handbag, its base pressed against her bosom. Her cousin Celie's bag, for she had decided that she would not wear black, would not believe the worst. Navy-blue crimplene was smart and, she sighed, a good compromise and she wanted everything to match, to ensure that Arthur would

166

not feel ashamed of her. So particular he was — Always look your best, Mamma — with that fastidious flattening of lips against his teeth as he checked her clothes for the prize-giving at high school. Her boy did not want to know about his father, about the fathers of Jim and Evvie — men whom she remembered only as eerie, elongated shadows that fell now and again, accidentally, across the frowning or smiling faces of her children. She had barely begun her story, choked with shame, when he interrupted, Mamma, it's just you and us and let's not talk about it, let's not talk about anyone else. You've done everything by yourself. From nothing you started the shop and look now everything's okay. That's all I want to know. Or something like that, something that promised to wash away the shame of twenty years and from Arthur, her youngest, who was so particular. Too particular? That's what Celie thought, she knew what Celie-them thought, but no one would dare say anything to her.

From the start, from the very moment of his conception, there had been a weight in her womb which told of the specialness she was carrying, so that she hardly registered the disappearance of the man, the father. Or perhaps she had just come to expect it. But this time she didn't care. The foetus absorbed what little shock there was. She loved the child who lurched about wildly in her belly, a child who wanted to be born. No ambiguous flutterings in the womb; he moved purposefully and, three weeks before he was due, manoeuvred into position and fought his way out, a strong, healthy baby. If surprisingly slight. No ordinary boy, he; she knew that he would be a bank manager or a president or something even bigger, although she warned him against messing about with politics. Always particular he was, her Arthur. How, and Dorothy's fist beat at the pillows, how could they tell her that there was no trace of him, that he had just disappeared? Just a name? A missing person? An absence? A nothing? Oh, she felt the emptiness, the lightness that would make her body rise to that heaven-high ceiling and cackle at the nothingness that had been her soul snuffling against a handbag.

She grabbed the handbag, slipped on her shoes and coat and rushed out. She would not cry here in this barbarous place where no one cared to find his body. That was what the girl,Tsiki, had said. That they had done nothing: a tired police constable had arrived two days later to ask obscure questions and did not come back. That it was a conspiracy, but she did not know what that could mean. She would find her child and she boldly hailed a taxi, one that stood right outside the door, as if it were waiting for her, to take her to the Botanic Gardens.The man did not say Ma'am; he asked for money and shrugged and shook his head and just held out his hand when she said British Council. He joked about her twenty-pound note — Lots of money eh — and gave her as change a ten-pound note with a picture of what seemed to be smiling Africans. Something was written across the image in blue ball-point pen. This taxi driver was not to be trusted. To hell with blooming mysteries and secret codes. Politics was one thing, but joke currency quite another. For ten years she had been running her own village shop successfully; a business woman was not to be fooled in this way.

Listen, man, here in England the notes say Bank of England, she said, and in response to his frown, added, No good sitting there with a mouthful of teeth; if you've got something to tell me why don't you speak? I'm a shopkeeper; I trade groceries for cash; don't think you can cheat me with signs and codes, and checking the other side of the note, or false money from some Clydesdale Bank.

The man engaged a gear as he hissed, Just you fuck off, Missus. Bank of England! Where do you think you are? This isn't fucking England, and drove off.

But surely Scotland was part of England ... *Ag*, she couldn't understand these people; she would have to speak to the official man in the kilt and if there were any problem with the money, perhaps he could sort it out.

The Kibble Palace was a fairy-tale house of glass and wrought iron painted silver. In the first, smaller dome the distant crown of a palm tree brushed against the glass top. There at the top, each row of panes grew narrower, tapering until the tiny rectangles of glass turned into sharp triangles, which would, had there been sunlight, sparkle like diamonds. Fat, orange fish floated in the pond at the base of the tree. It was warm. She sat on a wooden bench, one she was sure Arthur would have sat on. It was no doubt the heat that had brought him here so often. But she would not give in to grief, would not allow her heart to howl with pain. She would get to the bottom of this; she owed it to Arthur who never, never would have killed himself.

She took out the ten-pound note. On the front, where a picture of a man called David Livingstone was trapped amongst palm leaves, it claimed to be issued by Clydesdale Bank plc. On the back — and she flushed with shame — a naked woman was flanked on either side by naked men, captives or slaves, squatting serenely in their leg-irons under palm trees. An overdressed Arab on a camel occupied the middle-ground, whilst in the distance a sailing boat drifted on the water. Across the picture and across the plain white strip at the edge marked simply with the £10 figure, someone, the taxi-man perhaps, had written in blue pen: if dat bastard Geldof don't git ere soon I goes eat dat camel.

Dorothy smoothed the note and put it into her wallet, carefully, in order not to crease it. What was she to make of this message? And who would write such bad English on what she now had to believe was a perfectly good note? A visiting dominee had once explained about the Bible, how the stories meant something other than what the actual words said. Then the story about the leper, which he explicated, turned out to mean exactly what she had always thought it to mean and she checked with Mrs Willemse who said the same. So, if one thing did stand for another, she was perfectly capable of working it out. But which figure was she to attribute the words to? Livingstone, an explorer, she remembered, but could he really be showing off his slaves? And who was Geldof? Should she substitute Arthur for Geldof, which was surely a Boer name? And *geld* meaning money? She shook her head, bewildered. And the word 'bastard' — that she supposed was to show that they knew everything about Arthur. If Arthur were the victim, to be ... oh, she would not think the monstrous thing through. The British Council man was right. She had to keep going, keep moving. The horror thickened in the heat but she steadied herself and carried on.

In the approach to the main dome, on either side of the glass corridor, a discreet notice announced that this was South Africa. Not that she recognised many of the plants. A raggedy tree labelled Greyia seemed familiar but the Erica tree, sprinkled with icing-sugar, she had certainly never seen before. It was blossom: a million miniature white chalices with the slenderest of brown stamens. Camellia japonica flowered a deep pink that Arthur loved. He would have come in from the biting cold into this brilliance of heat and colour and recognised, perhaps from his books, the lilies, nerine, strelitzia, agapanthus and of course the hen-and-chickens posing under a posh name. She said the names of the flowers aloud in Arthur's measured tone. And she heard his new black shoes on the floor of bricks packed into neat chevrons as he followed the lure of the heat into the dome.

Palm trees squashed together in the inner circle and from the wrought-iron beams drops of condensation plopped into the dome of silence. Dorothy unbuttoned her coat. She turned right into the outer circle through Australia, New Zealand, a South American jungle, the undergrowth of temperate Asia, the Canaries and the Mediterranean. How quickly it took to tread the entire world, for in no time she was back at the icing-sugared Erica, entering South Africa once again.

It was in his fourth letter that Arthur spoke of lithops, of the hot stony beds where they kept prickly pears and other succulents. She found the room and smiled at the Namaqua vygies, made up like *platteland* girls in Town, sitting pertly behind glass if you please. But she knew nothing of the reed-and-timber hut that beckoned from another room. Its walls were lined with boards displaying texts and photographs of the Trades House of the Glasgow Expedition to Papua New Guinea. There were pictures of bearded white men with rucksacks walking through forests or bending over indistinguishable plants. Then Dorothy gasped, for there, before her very eyes, was Arthur, poring over a table of uprooted plants. His spread right hand was held out as if in blessing over the collection. The caption called him the High Commissioner for Papua New Guinea. Dorothy held onto the wooden post. Oh, she could have sworn it was Arthur, her own boy, tall and slender, but she supposed the man was somewhat older. Why was this photograph of a black man mounted here to break her heart? She would not look again at this High Commissioner, and she felt a chill creep up from her feet and spread through her entire body. But she carried on, now stiff with cold. As the man from the British Council said, there was nothing to do but to carry on. She read out the text on the next board, loudly, like a child learning to read:

... to seek out orchids, begonias and ferns for display at the Glasgow Garden Festival and, thereafter, to become part of the permanent collection maintained at the Glasgow Botanic Gardens, part of the cultural heritage of the City.

Dorothy sank to the earth floor of the Papua New Guinea hut, leaned her head against a wooden post and spread out her legs comfortably. A young child came upon her and skipped to and fro between those legs and shouted, Mu-um, look a *Papoo* person. But his mother whispered, Shush, and dragged him away. It was ten minutes later that a guard took her by the arm and lifted her to her feet. She did not brush the dust from her navy-blue coat. What did it matter? She knew Arthur had been swallowed by this city, that he would never again pick a thread from her lapel. Always look your best, Mamma. Always look your best — so she lifted her head, held it up. But she could not answer the uniformed man's questions. He spoke softly, kindly, and she handed over her handbag to him. So he called a taxi which took her back to the hotel.

Months later, leaning over the shop counter and peering into the heart of a cloud shaped like a camel, Dorothy could have sworn that the man had spoken to her in Afrikaans. Why did she remember the words *'Alles sal regkom, Mevrou'*, but she could of course not be sure.

Another Story

Approaching D.F. Malan airport. The view from the window on the right, that is, as you enter the aircraft: it falls out of the blue, suddenly, even with your eyes fixed on the ground rising towards you — a perfect miniature plane, a razor-edged shadow in the last of the sunlight, earth-borne, yet flying alongside where before there had been nothing. And then it grows. Because the sun is low and because nothing, no nothing, will remain a little toy-thing. (A darling little toy-thing, but that sort of word has no place here, and must be excised.) Yes, flying across the earth, it gradually grows larger. Still wonderful while its outline remains sharp, until an ungainly leap in size when overblown, with edges grown soft and arrowed wings blunted, the once-lovely little thing spreads and is swallowed. A simple multiplication and division sum, a working out of velocity, height, angle of the sun, etc. could have foreseen that moment. So that was that. And the plane landed with the usual bump and the ping of the pilot's intercom. But she didn't. Or perhaps couldn't.

To tell the truth, Miss Kleinhans was scared. And Dollie's voice, as she leaned over the wild-with-morning-glory fence, rang in her ears.

If you asking my advice, Deborah Kleinhans, I say stay right here where you belong. You not young, man, and there is no need to go gallivanting after family you don't know from Adam. Family is now family, but the whole point is that family is family because you know them and all their tricks. It's not about a stranger who gets to know you through ink and how-do-you-do on paper. And

173

remember Cape Town is full of troubles with people throwing stones and getting shot. And what with you being a stranger there in Town — have you listened to the wireless today?

Deborah's head spun in an attempt to work out how knowing or not knowing blood relations affected the claims that such people could legitimately make on her, for she had come to see the visit as a duty. Also, the morning-glory trumpets had started yawning, and she watched the first fold up neatly, spiralling into a tight spear that betrayed nothing of its fulsome blue.

Dollie, this business will take some thinking about, but another time; it's too cold out here for me, she had said tartly.

Deborah had not asked for Dollie's advice; she had only said how she couldn't decide. But, if only she'd listened to Doll who was after all a sensible person, a neighbour one could rely on, even if that husband of hers was a good-for-nothing *dronklap*. I should have been a spinster like you hey, Dollie sometimes said in exasperation, but Deborah could tell how the word 'spinster' cut into her heart, for Doll would swirl the remains of her coffee and gulp down the lot as she rose with just that hint of hoarseness in her voice. She would have to go and get ready the old man's *bredie*. Or his socks, or boots, or ironing, and even Deborah, the spinster, knew that that was not the worst a woman had to do. She who had worked for years in white households knew more about the world than people thought.

There had been two letters, the first simply a matter of introduction. A certain Miss Sarah Lindse from a wayward branch had traced her, a great-aunt, wishing to check the family connection, and with Old Testament precision had untangled the lines of begetting into a neat tree that Deborah nevertheless found hard to follow. Coloured people didn't have much schooling in her day but she knew her Bible, and there was no better education in the world than knowing that Good Book from

174

cover to cover. Still, enough names on those heavy branches looked familiar, although, so many children, dear Lord, why ever did her people have so very many children. Family tree! It was a thicket, a blooming forest in which the grandest of persons would get lost. And she pursed her mouth fastidiously: she had a lot to be thankful for.

There were times when you had to face the truth, times like this when you'd made the wrong decision and the Goodlord allowed you the opportunity to say, I've been guided by vanity. But in the same breath Deborah found her vindication: for a person who had worked as a respectable housekeeper all her life, but in service all the same, the connection with this grand young woman was only what she deserved. A history teacher at the grand University of Cape Town. No doubt to do with the drop of white blood, but she sighed as she thought of that blood — pink and thin and pure trouble. *Ag*, that was a long time ago, and now she had a niece, a lovely girl who was educated and rich and who wrote in the second letter, Why not come and have a holiday in Cape Town? I'll send you a plane ticket. To her, an old woman whom the child had never even met. And Deborah, who had been timid all her life, who kept her feet firmly on the ground and her eyes modestly fixed on those feet, for once looked up to see the serpent of adventure wink through the foliage of that family tree. And she was undone. And at her age too. But she replied, keeping with a steady hand to the lines of the Croxley pad although these modern pens behaved as if light upward strokes and bold downward strokes were the last thing they hoped to achieve: I have always wanted to fly and would like to look around Cape Town. But I don't need a holiday so you can save up the darning and the sewing and I could also do the cooking while you get on with bookwork. Thank you for the offer.

It was, of course, that advice of Dollie's that set her on the wrong path. Deborah had managed to think it through, and it simply did not make sense. Family is *mos* family, and the whole point of such an unnecessary statement is that you don't have to know the person. Vanity again: she had proven her ability to reason things out for herself, and in showing off to Dolly had brought upon herself this business, this anxiety.

If only there were someone to talk to on the aeroplane. Silence was something lovely and still when you were on your own, but here, with a flesh-and-blood person sitting right by your side, the silence fidgets between you, monitors your breathing, stiffens the body and makes you fearful of moving. So many new things can't become part of you unless you could say to the person sitting right there: My what a business this is, without of course letting on that you've never flown before. But the red-faced woman next to her had swung round to the aisle as if she, Deborah Kleinhans, freshly bathed and in her best crimplene two-piece, as if she had BO. *Ag*, it's the way of the world, she consoled herself, these posh people don't know how to work things out, can't even run their own blooming homes. If she were in charge she'd have apartheid to serve the decent and God-fearing — that was a more sensible basis for separating the sheep from the goats, but she sighed, for how would one know, how could one tell the virtuous from the hypocrites, the Pharisees. These days people grew more and more like jackals, and the education business only helped to cover up sorcery and ... and ... fornication, that was the word. These days she did not always find the right word.

And now Deborah felt once more a twinge of regret, a tugging at her intestines, which, fortunately, could be diverted from the foolish venture to the wonderful South African Airways lunch. All nicely separated into little compartments, she would explain to Dolly, her with the eternal *bredies*, day after day everything mixed together, meat, potatoes, tinned peas, vegetables, and then, on the plate, that man of hers would stir in the rice, pounding all together, as if it were mortar to be shovelled into the cracks of his soul. Oh, it would've been nice just to say

176

something to the red-faced woman. She would say: Isn't it *oulik*, the little brown dishes like housie-housie things? Last time I flew they were orange, you know. Just in case. And she lifted her head high; no one could accuse her, Miss Kleinhans, of being ignorant, green and *verskrik* like a young farm-girl. The Goodlord, she felt sure, would forgive the little white lie, especially after the temptation, the terrible desire to put a dish in her bag, only the little pudding dish of brown and cream plastic, and with the white woman's back virtually turned to her nothing could have been easier. But she didn't. And she praised Dearjesus who resisted forty days in the wilderness, and felt sure that He would not expect her to fast just because He had, not on this her first flight with food so prettily packed in their separate dishes.

That was before Deborah thought of the order of eating. She knew that one didn't start just any old where you liked. Her De Villiers household always had fish or soup to begin, but with neither on this tray, how was she to determine the order of things that were much the same? It was a test that would have made the white woman, if her back had not mercifully been turned, giggle at her ignorance, for there in one of the little dishes was tomato and lettuce alone, and in another again tomato and lettuce but with meat, and how was she to decide which came first? More than likely two halves of the same tomato given different names in different containers, which only went to show how silly this blinking business was. And at what point was she to eat the round bread?

Deborah flushed; she was grateful for the disdain of the woman who had swung round towards the aisle. She remembered that her father always said that only poor people ate bread with their dinner, so she would look upon it as another test, like in a fairy tale about a round red apple or something like that to catch the heroine out. Why else would the two large blackberries have been hidden under the lettuce? She would have arranged it on top to set off the green and red nicely; she had always paid attention to presenting food nicely, and Mrs De Villiers never had anything but praise for her dishes.

The pip of the foul-tasting berry proved yet another trap. How was she to get the damned thing out of her mouth and back onto the plate? Would she have to pretend that she was not hungry, that she could only just pick at her food? What nonsense, she admonished herself. This was no boiled sweet that would dissolve; she could not very well keep a stone hidden in her cheek until God-knows-when, so she spat it into a paper napkin under cover of wiping her mouth, and niftily tucked it into her sleeve. There was no one watching her; she would tuck in and not waste the poor girl's money. This food — never mind that it didn't live up to the cute containers — was expensive, and what's more, paid for. How could she, a grown person, be so silly, and she chuckled audibly so that the red-faced woman took the opportunity to shift in her seat, to straighten her spine and allow herself ten degrees that would bring Miss Kleinhans's fork just within her line of vision.

The girl must be relying on a family resemblance, for why else had she not suggested ways of identifying herself? Perhaps she should wave a white handkerchief or something. That was what people did in the *Rooi Rose* stories, which only went to show that *Rooi Rose* then was not for people like her. Deborah could never do such a thing, make a spectacle of herself. It must have been the flight through high air that made her even think of such a strange thing. As if she had taken a feather duster to her head so that those stories, she now clearly saw, were for white people. Which, of course, didn't mean that she couldn't read them: she was used to wearing white people's clothes and eating their leftovers, so what difference did it make reading their stories? As long as she knew and did not try to behave like a *Rooi Rose* woman. It was difficult enough just sitting there, waiting, with so many idle eyes roving about. She lifted her head to concentrate on the lights flashing their instructions about smoking and seat belts and things until they finally clicked off, the messages exhausted, and felt herself adrift midst empty seats and the purposeful shuffle of people anxious to get away.

Deborah looked about and caught sight of the red-faced woman who flashed her a warm smile. What on earth could the person mean by that? She was not to be lured by a smile of falsehood, here where there was no danger of striking up a conversation. As far as she was concerned it was just too bladdy late. What a cheek, but then, not keeping track of things, a smile leaked from her lips all the same, and she had no choice but to incline her head to nod a greeting.

The usual Cape Town wind awaited her, just as Dollie had said, and Deborah smoothed her skirt and patted her head to check that the *doekie* was still in place. Crossing that space was not simply a matter of putting one foot before another. The tarmac felt sticky underfoot; the wind snapped like a mongrel, and her ankles wobbled unreliably above the Sunday shoes. Ahead, through the glass, a tinted crowd waited, waved, and what would she do if the girl were not there? That she could not allow herself to think about. The Goodlord would provide. Although the Goodlord so often got His messages mixed up, like telephone party-lines, so that good fortune would rain into the unsuspecting lap of that heathenish husband of Dollie's, when it was she, Deborah Kleinhans, who had spent the holy hours on arthritic knees, praying. If red-face, walking purposefully just ahead of her, was expecting no one, you could be sure that some thoughtful niece had on the spur of the moment decided to meet her after all, while she, a stranger in this town ... But this time, and Deborah was careful to smile inwardly, this time, He got it just right.

Sarah was sure that she would recognise her great-aunt by a family resemblance, and indeed the woman walking unsteadily across the tarmac could be no other than Deborah Kleinhans. Who, incidentally, was the only elderly coloured woman on the flight. Sarah corrected herself: so-called coloured, for she did not think that the qualifier should be reserved for speech. It grieved her that she so often had to haul up the 'so-called' from some distant recess where it slunk around with foul words like half-caste and half-breed, and she stamped her foot, which had gone to sleep in the long wait, as if to shake down the unsummoned words. Lexical vigilance was a matter of mental hygiene, a regular rethinking of words in common use, like cleaning out rotten food from the back of a refrigerator where no one expects food to rot and poison the rest.

The old woman was stronger, sturdier than she had imagined, with the posture of someone much younger. But she was tugging at the navy-blue suit which had got nipped, perhaps by her roll-on corset, so that her hemline dipped severely to the right. Also, threatening to slip off was the matching *doekie* which had to be hauled back over the grey head as she struggled with a carrier-bag in the wind. But they met without difficulty.

So we found each other. Something to be grateful for these days when you lose and search for things that disappear under your very nose ...

And people going missing by the dozens, Sarah interjected.

Deborah looked alarmed. Whatever was the child talking about; not her, she had to get back home; Dollie would be expecting her in precisely one week.

Ag, they say big cities swallow you up but we're old enough to look after ourselves. Dollie's people, she added, even in Kimberley, you know, after the riots — clean disappeared. But one never knows with these young people. Dollie is now Mrs Lategan who's been my neighbour for twenty years. Then she chuckled. But what if we are not the people we think we are, or no, that's not what I mean. Let's sit down, my girl, I get so *deurmekaar*, and I need to have a good look at you.

They sat down and looked at each other surrounded by squeals and hugs and arm-waving reunions. In the two pairs of eyes, the green-flecked hazel eyes derived from the same sockets of a long-dead European missionary, there was nothing to report. The improbable eyes, set generations ago into brown faces, betrayed nothing, as eyes rarely do, but both claimed to read in the other signs and traces, so that they held each as firmly as the rough and wrinkled hand gripped the young and smooth. Deborah wondered for the first time why the girl had brought her all that way. Sarah thought of her father who in his last years had clung to a miscellany of rare physical complaints. A man who knew his viscera like the back of his hand and could identify a pain or chill with self-claimed accuracy — in the tip of his liver, or pancreas, or lower section of the colon — an unnecessary refinement since the remedy of *buchu* essence served them all. She hoped that her great-aunt would not get ill; those were surely the eyes of a hypochondriac.

The girl was rather disappointing, untidily dressed in denim without as much as a dash of lipstick to brighten her up. There was something impenetrable about her face, a density of flesh that thwarted Deborah who prided herself on looking right into the souls of strangers. Also, her car was not at all what Deborah expected, but then she did not think any car smart except for a black one. The house that they pulled up at was very nice, but modest, she thought, for a learned person. With so much rain here in Cape Town it seemed a pity not to have a proper garden. Just a little patch of untrimmed grass and a line of flowers sagging against the wall. Yellow and orange marigolds, their heads like torches, so that she turned to look back at the dark mountain and saw the last light gathered in the flaming peak of a cloud.

The medicinal scent of marigolds followed them into the house. Through the passage lined with old photographs. So many people with nothing better to do than stand around and wait for the click of a camera. And right into the kitchen, until the marigolds gave in to the smell of coffee. From a blue enamel pot like her very own the girl poured large cupfuls, and Deborah's heart leapt, for city people she thought drank only instant coffee, didn't have time for a Koffiehuis brew. Washed in well-being, she felt her feet throb all the more painfully so that she eased off her shoes to find two risen loaves straining under the nylon stockings. It's the flight, Sarah explained. But why feeling good should have alerted her to feeling bad, Deborah did not know, but oh she felt like a queen being led to her room with a bowl of hot water in which to soak those feet. But queens get their heads chopped off, so it was not surprising that as she rested before dinner, in a dream-wake state, Deborah orbited wildly in a marigold-round, her eyes chasing the pinpoints of light where orange turned to fire and her head threatening to fly off. She rose, clutching her throat.

At table Sarah talked too much. Deborah, used to turning her own thoughts slowly around, this way and that, and then putting them away safely for another inspection day, found the girl's insistent ways too exhausting. Like Mr De Villiers's office with rows and rows of narrow drawers packed with papers — the girl's head, it would seem, was like that. And she spoke fast, whirring like a treadle-machine that made Deborah's own head, still delicate from dreaming, spin once again. And all these things from the past, the bad old days that Sarah wanted to talk about — stories folded and packed in mothballs right at the bottom of Deborah's head. To disturb those was just plain foolish, just asking for the world to come toppling down.

Perhaps later this year I'll come to Kimberley, to look around all those places. The old farm, Brakvlei — all those places where the Kleinhanses lived, Sarah said.

But the old woman would not be roused. Nothing there to see, not a coloured person left in those parts. You won't find a *riempie* or a rusty nail. No, it's years since I left, and soon after that the others trekked — the drought, you know. Girlie, this is now a lovely *bobotie*. I haven't had any for so long: being on your own you can't really make such elaborate food.

The girl was not a bad cook, considering. And the *bobotie* was good, although Deborah liked it just a bit sweeter, just another spoonful of apricot jam to set off the sharpness of the dried apricots. That's what she liked about *bobotie* — the layers, different things arranged on top of each other. She always did it in a nice Pyrex dish so that you could see the separate layers of curried mince, apricots, and then the thick custard just trickling down, down through the dried fruit. Almost a pity to eat such a lovely thing.

No really, she said through slipping dentures, there's nothing like a good *bobotie*. Bananas are also good you know, but to contrast with the custard, apricot is best.

In the tall frosted glass of Fanta the orange bubbles broke merrily at the brim, almost too pretty to drink. On the same principle, Deborah's good clothes remained in the cupboard, unworn. But today, in her Sunday wear, eating and drinking, bathing in the beauty of it all, her old heart was content, and this Sarah was a girl to be proud of. She would bring Dollie along next year; my, what a time they would have. Then Sarah said in a preacher's voice: nothing but an untidiness on God's earth ... a mixture of degenerate brown peoples, rotten with sickness, an affront against Nature ... So that was the farm.

They had slipped into comfortable Afrikaans, a relief to Deborah whose English pinched like the Lycra step-in that Dollie insisted had to be worn for the visit. Why on earth should the girl have switched again, so that Deborah now had to grope and grunt, for the two languages flew at each other to make wild words; she just could not understand about this sickness and death, and so she felt a great weariness, a cloud settling around her head. The girl was surely mad. Everybody gets sick and dies, but Brakvlei was never rotten. Oh no, theirs was the cleanest of farmyards, the stony *veld* swept for hundreds of yards and even the fowls knew not to shit near the house. In that swept yard a young man rested his brown arms on the latched lower door, leant well into the dark but spotless kitchen with the sun behind him lighting the outline of his tightly curled hair. And Deborah, sick with shyness, packed more wood into the full stove and felt her hem a hot hoop below her knees, for she had outgrown that dress, and she had never been looked at in that way. Even when he offered to cleave a log that refused to go into the stove, his eyes burned, and then her Pa came in to see his favourite daughter — his miracle late-lamb, younger than the grandchildren — tug at her skirt, and he ordered Andries away. That day she tore the dress into rags and braved a beating, for she knew that a strip of plain cotton would simply have been sewn on to lengthen the skirt. But a beating has never done anyone any harm and she could thank her Pa now for sitting here where the girl's strong hands came to rest on her shoulders.

Auntie feeling alright? Perhaps a little drop of *buchu* essence? she asked, once again in Afrikaans.

No I'm okay. Just put a tiny little bit of *bobotie* on my plate.

Then Deborah remembered the slanderous words about the farm. Cleanliness is next to godliness, that's what my mother always said. And it was my job every morning to sweep all around the house. Really it was just a question of rearranging the veld, making our own patterns of earth and stone with the grass broom, but she said the *veld* will swallow us up if we don't sweep. No my child, you can ask anyone: Brakvlei was the tidiest little place you've ever seen. If your people think otherwise, well, then they just don't know what tidy means. And all my life I've kept that motto: tidiness is next to godliness.

And then her anger subsided. Her mother would not have quoted the saying in English as she had just done, no, not at home. What had she in fact said? How unreliable words were, lodging themselves comfortably in the memory where they pretended to have a rightful place.

Deborah did not hold her memory responsible. A question of too many languages, if you asked her, even on TV nowadays, all these new black languages.

No, no, Sarah soothed, I'm sure you're right. I have no doubt that Brakvlei was well kept. But I wasn't really talking about Brakvlei; it was just something I remembered — from a story.

But the young woman's eyes burned so bright, so much the busybody, that Deborah recognised the passion for probing deep into other people's affairs. Who did this child think she was, wanting to pry into her life, and she who had never said a word to anyone — no not even to Dollie — about Andries, the tall young man whom she saw just once more before her father, waving the old shotgun, told him not to set foot in that swept yard again.

People come and people go, and in the end it's no bad thing. No point in brooding over things that happened a long time ago. I haven't got time for those old stories, she said firmly.

A pity really; it's an interesting story that needs to be told ...

And what would you know about it? Deborah interrupted. It's never been interesting. Dreary as dung it was, sitting day after day waiting for something to happen, listening for hooves or the roll of cartwheels.

She checked herself. Hearing only the wind howl through the bushes and the ewes bleat, she had made up stories — of driving through streets lined with whitewashed houses; of friends, girls in frilled print frocks who whispered secrets under the breath of the wind; and of Andries on horseback galloping across the swept yard right up to the kitchen door. But she said, You know I have my books — *Rooi Rose* every fortnight, I haven't missed a book since I started working for the De Villierses, and when I retired I kept it up. Every fortnight. Good stories that seem to be about real life, but well, when you think about it, you won't recognise anyone you know. They give you no useful tips. They're no better than the nonsense I used to make up in my own head to kill the time. My advice, child, is to stick to your business and forget about stories of old times.

It depends surely on who tells the story. Auntie Deborah, that's what I must ask you about. Do you know if someone has written the story of our family, from the beginning, right from the missionary from Europe? Do you know of a woman, a white woman, speaking to your mother or brothers about those old days? A woman who then wrote a book about them? Have you heard of such a book? Of...

No, I don't believe it. What nonsense. Of course there was no such woman, no such thing. A book for all to read with our dirty Kleinhans washing spread out on snow white pages? *Ag* no man, don't worry; it wouldn't be our story; it's everyone's story. All coloured people have the same old story. Not worth writing a book about. And then Deborah slumped in her chair.

Sarah knew it — just her luck, the old woman travelling all this way to put down her head and die at her table. She held a bottle of brandy to the lifeless lips. The eyelids fluttered and Deborah sat up with remarkable agility, as if the laying of her head on the table had been a deliberate gesture of exasperation.

Just tired, child. Don't worry, I'm not going to die here; I'll die respectably in my own house, and that's not for some time yet.

Sarah helped her to bed. Tomorrow evening, she said, as she tucked her in, I have to go to a meeting. But in the morning we'll go out. Somewhere exciting, but let's talk about that tomorrow.

To the Gardens, girlie, that's where one should go first. I've heard so much about the grand Gardens in Cape Town where the fine ladies parade. And she giggled for she knew it could not be as her mother had described so many years ago. And even then it was a second-hand account, told by her grown-up sister Elmira whom she, Deborah, had never known.

Deborah was not surprised by the knock. Her heart had swollen, filling her chest with a thunderous beat and rocking her entire body as she heard the footsteps steal past her window, round to the back of the house. *Skollies* with armfuls of stones, just as Dollie had warned her. Then a low voice, barking, Quick. Here.

Slowly Deborah twisted her head to look at the clock. Then she leapt out of bed. She would not await death like this, cowardly and prone. Oh no, if *skollies* planned to kill her, well, they would find her standing up straight, ready to meet her Maker. Her hands groped for the dressing gown, but the old arms shook too violently to be guided through the sleeves. She crept out to the hall; she could at least telephone the police. But they were already at the door. What kind of cheeky *skollies* were these who thought she would open the door to her own death? Why did the girl not wake up? The knock grew louder and someone shouted, Open up. Police. Police. They had come for Sarah.

Deborah waited for Dollie in the Lategans' kitchen. Mr Lategan put the kettle on for coffee, making an elaborate display of not knowing where to find things, so that she suggested he put on his shoes while she made the coffee. That the man should be told to make himself decent, as if she would divulge a thing to someone sitting in his socks. And she thought of the folly of having expectations, of how she had imagined sitting at that table with Dollie, telling her story.

But there they sat drinking the coffee she had made, and Mr Lategan knew exactly where to find Dollie's buttermilk rusks, which they dunked. And so she told him, for she could not expect the man to ask again. About the police who came for Sarah at five-thirty in the morning, pointing their guns as if they were in a play on the TV. And how they turned the house upside down, and even looked through her suitcase. But they were very polite, especially the big one in command who apologised nicely and said to her she should have kept an eye on the girl, so that she turned on him triumphantly and said how he didn't know everything like he said he did, how she'd known the girl for less than a day. Mr Lategan interrupted to say that if they didn't know the simple facts, they could so easily have got the whole business wrong, the wrong house, the wrong woman, the wrong everything. Which was exactly what Deborah was about to say, also the wrong Deborah Kleinhans, for she felt as if the story had been playing on the TV, but she allowed him to make the point.

There was also Cape Town to tell about, even though she knew that he had been there twice. But the city was so big that he could not possibly have visited the same places, and he certainly listened with great interest. Sarah had written a letter to her neighbours, the Arendses, and even then Deborah marvelled at the girl's skill, how she wrote like lightning, her hand flying across the paper in such straight lines, even though the big policeman leant rudely over her, checking every word. Busybodies, that's what they were, going through people's things, ladies' things too, and reading their letters. Mrs Arendse took her to the Gardens but her heart was not in it. Someone else, a young woman whose name she could not recall, took her to a museum to see what the girl called their ancestors. Hottentots in a big glass box, squatting around an unlit fire of all things, so that she left in disgust. (But she said nothing to Mr Lategan about the large protruding buttocks and the shameful loincloths of animal skin.) No, her heart was not in it, and Mrs Arendse arranged an early return flight for there was no point in waiting to see Sarah again. They telephoned many, many times, but there was no point, everyone said. Sarah, she assured Mr Lategan, was nothing less than a decent, respectable, educated girl.

When Dollie came she told it all again and she did not mind the man sitting there — until he tried to correct her. If things were slightly different the second time round, well, she was telling it to someone different, and he should have had the decency to keep quiet. So she left, taking her bag, for she had not yet been home, and Dollie shouted after her, I'll come with, just as she unlocked her door.

Dollie lay across her bed as she unpacked. The frock for parading in the Gardens, a bold print of yellow daisies on white, she folded away into a bottom drawer for the nights were drawing in and really it was perhaps too bright for someone of her age. And then she told Dollie, of how she had offered to make a nice pot of coffee because it was so early and it was just what you needed in order to think clearly. If the policemen burst rudely into the house, well, she was brought up decently. Sarah shouted at her, but she knew how a civilised person ought to behave. And Deborah paused in an attempt to trace the moment when things became muddled, but all she recalled was the unmistakable smell of marigold, a weariness, and the precise timbre of the sergeant's voice as she finished pouring the coffee: Milk and sugar for the other two, but just black and bitter for me. Then without thinking, without anticipating the violence of the act, Deborah Kleinhans took each cup in turn and before his very eyes poured the coffee into the sink. Together they watched the liquid splash, a curiously transparent brown against the shiny stainless steel.

Acknowledgements

Many thanks to Roger Palmer whose artwork inspired the story "The one that got away". "Boy in a jute-sack hood" was published in *Antigonish Review* 150 (2008). The following all appeared first in a slightly different format: "Nothing like the wind" in *Stand* Vol 5.4 (2004); "N2" in *Stand* Vol 1.2 (1999); "In the Botanic Gardens" in *Landfall*, 176 (1990); "Another story" in *Colours of a New Day*, S. Lefanu & S. Hayward (eds.), Penguin Books (1991). "Raising the tone" is also published in *South of South*, edited by Nii Ayikwei Parkes (Peepal Tree, 2011).

I am grateful to the Bogliasco Foundation for a wonderful residency at their Liguria Study Centre.

I gratefully acknowledge the Research Leave supported by the Arts and Humanities Research Council (UK).  Arts & Humanities Research Council